MW00938810

The Blackout

Stephanie Erickson

Copyright © 2012 Stephanie Erickson

All rights reserved.

This is a work of fiction. Any names, characters, places and incidents are products of the author's imagination, or are used fictitiously. Any resemblance to actual events, locales or persons, living or dead, is entirely coincidental.

ISBN: 1481033247

ISBN-13: 978-1481033244

CONTENTS

Calm

1.

"The nature of the world is to be calm, and enhance and support life, and evil is an absence of the inclination of matter to be at peace."
– Gregory Maguire, <u>Wicked: The Life and Times of the Wicked Witch of the West</u>

What a difference one hundred years can make. The 20th century saw the dawn of automobiles, the Internet, cell phones and the personal computer. All of which came to rely on one common denominator – electricity.

The world hummed and clicked away, consuming more electricity than those who lived a century ago would have ever dreamed could exist. But it was a fragile existence, one easily shattered by the sun's fiery tendrils.

The light the world created blinded them. A storm was coming that would sweep across the globe like wildfire, leaving nothing but darkness in its wake.

2.

Molly was just finishing cleaning out her inbox when Cindy's slender frame walked by the door. "Hey!" Molly called out.

Cindy stopped and poked her head in. "Hey yourself. What's up?"

"Nothing. I'm just finishing up here, and was going to get some dinner. Wanna come?"

Cindy knew Molly was lonely and didn't get much social contact when her husband was gone. Even though she had a lot to do, Molly needed her. "Sure! The kids don't need to be picked up for a while, but I'm not quite ready to go yet. Can ya' wait like fifteen or twenty minutes?"

Molly smiled. Cindy was never quite ready to go. She had three kids and a sociable husband, so grading essays and preparing for the next class weren't easily accomplished at home.

"Sure, that sounds great. Just holler when you're ready."

Molly, on the other hand, had lots of quiet time at home. Gary had already been gone for two nights and wouldn't be back for another five. If nothing else, being a pilot's wife left her with plenty of time to herself. It was an adjustment she hadn't fully mastered, and she was grateful she wouldn't be eating alone tonight.

When Cindy left, Molly sifted through the night's work, thinking she'd get a head start. She opened the file for her Modern Poetry class and took out the essay on top. "Mutability", it was titled.

What can a person rely on? Friends and lovers come in and out of a person's life as often as they change their underwear.

Oh Lord, she thought, and flipped to the end of it. *Seven pages of this crap?* She leaned back in her chair, pulled off her rimless glasses and rubbed her eyes; her habit when she didn't want to embark on the task at hand. She sighed and uncapped her purple pen (she never used red - she found it too harsh, too judgmental, and way too negative) attempting to ready herself for the potential garbage she was about to trudge through.

Four pages in, Cindy came to the rescue. She had pulled her long blonde hair back into a low ponytail and donned a gray blazer over her white blouse and khaki pants. She was always very put-together and stylish.

"Ready!" she announced. "Where do you want to go?"

"Thank God! This essay is a nightmare." Molly paused, considering the options. "You know if I was alone I'd just go up to McDonald's. So, what are you in the mood for?"

Cindy frowned and wrinkled her nose. "Not McDonald's. I don't know how you can stay so thin and eat there as much as you do."

"I don't eat there every day."

Cindy laughed. "I know, but still! If I'm going to eat that many calories, I want it to be worth it!"

They walked to the stairwell together. Molly never took the elevator, so if one of her friends wanted to walk with her, they had to take the stairs. The building was only two stories high, and the elevator was installed in 1967.

Molly didn't trust it to get her where she needed to go reliably.

"Whatever. McDonald's is delicious," Molly countered. "So, since you vetoed my suggestion, where do you want to go?"

"I'm thinking pizza. How about the Pizza Garden?"

They stepped outside and Molly assessed the situation. "It's a nice evening. Pizza Garden sounds great."

The restaurant was only a few blocks from the campus, so walking was a no-brainer. Although they were likely to see some of their students, The Pizza Garden – with its homemade pizzas and calzones oozing with cheese and garlic – was well worth the risk.

The walk through historic downtown was beautiful, with small shops and businesses on either side of the street. It was mid-October, and the temperature in northern Florida was ideal for an evening stroll.

Molly pulled her navy blue cardigan a bit tighter and crossed her arms, trying to keep pace with Cindy. Cindy was at least a head taller than Molly – as most people were – so she had to work to keep up with Cindy's stride.

"Good Lord. Some of my classes this term are so defiant," Cindy said. "They think everything is a negotiation. If I tell them I want a fifteen hundred-word paper on *Twelfth Night* they try to haggle me down to seven-fifty. I'm like, really? Fifteen hundred words isn't that many for a Lit major. So quit your whining and just do it! I can't believe they pull this crap with some of the other teachers. I know Terry wouldn't tolerate that. I mean, are they doing that to you?" Her pace quickened with her declining mood, and Molly struggled to keep up.

"Well no, but I don't think we have that many of the same-" Cindy cut her off.

"So, what is it about me, Molly? Do I look like I don't know how to teach the material? Do I look like I need a nineteen or twenty-year-old to swoop in and rescue me from the burden of teaching Shakespeare? What is it?"

She turned to Molly with unbridled frustration in her eyes as they walked, and Molly only met her gaze for a moment. Not because she was uncomfortable, but because she knew better than to not watch where she was going.

Molly chuckled a bit, but not at her. It was comical how passionate they were about their craft, and sometimes the students just didn't get it. Particularly those who took Shakespeare or Modern Poetry for an "easy elective." It was nearly impossible to get through to them, but it didn't stop most of the faculty from trying. It sounded to Molly like Cindy had ended up with an entire class of "easy electives".

"Cindy, you have to try not to take it so personally. Some kids want to get the best grade possible by doing the least amount of work. It's how they'll approach their whole lives. I'm sure you're not the first person they've tried that crap on, and you certainly won't be the last. You just have to stick to your guns and lay down the law. They'll learn by mid-terms not to try that stuff with you anymore."

Cindy sighed as they approached the hostess at The Pizza Garden. She was – of course – a student they both had. "Hey Dr. Nicholas. Dr. Bonham. Table for two?"

"Please, Shelly," Molly said, thankful to have remembered her name. There were only a few thousand students at the college, but Molly often had a hundred of them per semester, and this was her third year on the faculty.

Cindy smiled half-heartedly at the girl as she scooted into the cement bench across the table. "Your waiter will be right with y'all," Shelly said and walked away.

Cindy jumped right back into their conversation, despite the brief interruption. "It's hard not to take it personally, ya know? I mean, why take the class if you don't care at least a little bit about Shakespeare?"

Molly cleared her throat as a young man approached

the table. He didn't seem familiar to her, but that didn't mean he wasn't in Cindy's Shakespeare class. He had dark, curly hair bordering on messy and wore a white apron over his t-shirt and jeans. He set a basket of garlic bread on the table and asked what they would like to drink. Both ordered Sprite, which he took down and hurried away.

Cindy smiled devilishly. "Do you know that kid?"

"No, do you? I thought he might be in your Shakespeare class."

"No, he's not. Probably some other lazy kid."

"Well, now, that's not quite fair. He's working, isn't he?"

They bantered back and forth about the waiter's work ethic until he came back to take their order. They asked for a pepperoni pizza to share, and munched on the garlic bread while they waited.

"How are the kids? And Tom?" Molly asked between bites, debating about whether her breath would reach toxic levels before this meal was over.

"Good. Busy-busy, you know. Grace started soccer last weekend, so of course Melody wants to do it too- just because she has to do everything her big sister does, not because she has any genuine interest in soccer. Poor Malcolm is caught in the middle. He wants to do karate, so Tom and I are looking into it. I actually think Melody would be a pretty good dancer if she'd give it a chance, but Grace isn't into it, so she doesn't want to do it."

"Well, that's a phase. I mean really, Melody is only five, and Grace is what, eight or nine now?"

"Nine."

"Yeah, so of course Melody thinks she's super-cool and wants to do everything Grace does. It's only natural. And Malcolm is the only boy sandwiched between two sisters, so he has to be independent."

"I know you're right, it's just annoying. It's not like Melody can play on the same team as Grace or anything. I'm not sure she understands that."

Molly nodded. "Well, anything is possible to a five-year-old. Why not let her try it, and see how she likes it? She might hate it, and then you'll be back to ballet." She paused to take a drink of Sprite. "Honestly, I don't know how you do it. How do you find time for three very different sets of activities with three very different kids, plus have a social life with Tom? I mean really, by the time I get home, walk the dog and read through the backlog of essays I've got, plus skim through reading for the next day's classes, it's ten o'clock and time for bed!"

"Well," she smiled, "I'm amazing and that's all there is to it." She paused and raised her eyebrow. "Plus, I haven't crawled into bed at ten o'clock...ever! What are you, like eighty-five?"

Molly laughed. Shifting the conversation had been a good move; Cindy was in a much better mood.

Cindy cleared her throat. "So, where is Gary tonight?"

"Oh, uh, Philadelphia I think." Her voice lowered an octave as the joy went out of it.

"So, I guess he'll be gone for the weekend?" Cindy was treading on thin ice, and she knew it. But Molly was the kind of person who needed something to look forward to when she was alone, so Cindy pushed forward.

Molly frowned into her Sprite as she stabbed at the ice with her straw. "Yup."

"Maybe you want to come with me and get pedicures?"

Her face brightened. "That sounds great!"

Satisfied, Cindy picked up the last of bite her pizza. "Great."

They finished dinner on a high note and walked happily back to the campus together.

When Molly got to her scooter, Cindy shook her head. "When are you going to get a real car?"

"We have a real car. Gary's truck does just fine for regular stuff. This is perfect for getting me back and forth to school and for errands downtown. It's easier to park!"

Molly pulled her pink helmet out from under the seat and snapped it on. "Anyway, I don't have a litter that I need to cart around from point A to point B."

She laughed. "Point taken. Just be careful. I wouldn't want you to get smooshed by some delivery truck trying to navigate these narrow streets."

"I'm always careful. Have a great night at home, and tell everyone hi!"

"You too. How much longer until Gary comes home?"

"Five days!" Molly always knew exactly how much time was left on that clock.

Cindy laughed. "Not that you're counting."

Molly started the scooter's engine. "Oh, I'm totally counting! You would too!"

"True. Alright, see ya tomorrow!"

Molly waved as she walked the scooter back out of the spot and drove away.

It was long past dark when Molly got home. Luckily she'd remembered to leave a hall light on in the house. She hated coming home to a dark house. They lived in a totally safe neighborhood, but she'd seen one too many *Lifetime* movies. You never knew who could be hiding in the shadows – unless you left the lights on and there weren't any shadows to hide in.

Before she even got the door open she could hear Dug panting and whining excitedly on the other side. He whacked the door once or twice with his tail as Molly fumbled with her keys and briefcase. When she finally (well, finally for him; in actuality it was only a few seconds) got the door open, he paused for half a breath to make sure it was in fact his owner at the door, then launched into the nightly excitement ritual. It basically consisted of hopping around in a circle, stopping to jump up on whoever was just arriving home, then running to get a drink of water and repeat.

Dug was a small longhaired terrier mix whom Molly

always thought looked a bit like Benji. They'd rescued him almost four years ago now, and despite Molly's best efforts to break him of jumping on people when they came in the house, everything always went right out the window when Gary came home. Mostly because Gary was just as excited to see Dug as Dug was to see him.

Molly set everything on the counter, the excitement ritual following her all the way to the kitchen, and then turned to face Dug. He immediately sat down, barely managing to contain himself. Of course, she petted him and rewarded him for his "restraint."

"Where's Sally?" she asked him. Sometimes, like on the weekends, the animals were the only ones she would talk to all day, so she always spoke to them like they were people.

Pretty soon Sally walked lazily around the corner and meowed, proclaiming her distaste at Molly's absence. "Hey there, pretty girl."

Molly allowed herself about five minutes of playing with them before she set her mind to the tasks at hand. She needed to finish grading essays, get ready for tomorrow's classes, and still get into bed at a reasonable hour. It was already nearly seven o'clock.

When she walked through the living room, she was thrown by an odd splashing sound. It seemed to correspond with Dug's movements. He was splashing…in the living room. She looked around, trying to find the source of the water. It was just a thin layer, but it was everywhere. Then, she found it. The fish tank was empty, with tiny corpses lying at the bottom.

Her shoulders fell. *Dammit*, she thought.

Dug was totally oblivious to her peril as she sloshed across the living room to the kitchen, searching for a safe place to put her briefcase and papers. Once she'd unloaded on the kitchen table, she turned and stared at the mess.

Now what? she thought. *This crap always happens when I'm alone.* She frowned at the dark hardwood floors glistening at her through a thin layer of water, fighting tears. She took out her phone and snapped a picture of the mess.

This is what I came home to, she texted to Gary.

While she was going for the mop and bucket, he answered her. *What happened?*

Fish tank sprung a leak. All the fish are dead. :-(

Oh no! I'm so sorry I'm not there to help! That stinks honey! There were a lot of fish in there!

I know. She didn't know what else to say to him. She was frustrated and upset. She had work to do, and didn't have time to be cleaning water off the floor, let alone taking care of proper fish disposal.

It was slow work. Eventually, Dug settled down at the edge of the living room, after Molly repeatedly discouraged him from getting on the couch while he was wet. Sally simply watched from the safety of the stairs.

It took Molly all evening to get enough water off the floor to start drying it with towels. She just hoped the hardwood wasn't ruined, not to mention the baseboards and drywall.

Once she had towels spread all over the floor, Gary texted her again. *How's it going?*

She responded with another picture. It looked like a mess.

Gary, trying to be encouraging, said, *It's coming along!*

Indeed.

By the time she turned her attention to the dripping tank, she was exhausted. She unceremoniously gathered the fish with the net into a plastic bowl and flushed them, feeling like she should have said a few words or something. But she was so irritated and tired by then she couldn't come up with anything except, "thanks for ruining my night."

It was nearly eleven o'clock by the time she went upstairs to get showered and ready for bed. Her entire evening was wasted. She didn't get any of her papers read, and the students were expecting their grades tomorrow. Plus she had a headache from crying, which hadn't even made her feel better. She rolled her eyes as she climbed into the shower, trying to wash the last four hours of irritation away. Steam filled the bathroom and she sat on the shower floor until the water turned cold.

It was midnight by the time she'd brushed her teeth, dried her hair and climbed into bed. Exhausted, she mustered the energy for a quick call to Gary.

"Hey," he said when he answered.

"Hi."

"So, you had an exciting evening."

She ran her fingers through Dug's fur absentmindedly. "Yup."

"Didja get it all cleaned up?"

"For the most part. I can't get the tank out of there though. You'll have to help me with it."

"I might be able to patch it."

"Uh…" She hesitated. How could she express her feelings about cleaning up another mess without slighting her husband's ability? "We'll have to talk about that when you get home. How was your day?" She hoped a change in subject would mask the potential for insult.

"Fine. Uneventful. The passengers were late in Atlanta, so we missed lunch, thinking they were going to show up any minute. Then, because they were late, we didn't get to eat dinner until like seven. It was obnoxious." Gary often missed meals waiting for people. They had snacks on the airplane they could eat, so he wouldn't starve, but peanut butter M&Ms are still a far cry from a meal when you're hungry.

"Oh, I'm sorry, babe. Where to tomorrow?"

"Just Orlando. It's a one-leg kind of day, which is fine by me."

She yawned. "That sounds good."

"OK, I'll let you get some sleep. Meeting in the lobby at seven tomorrow morning, so I should start heading in that direction too."

"OK, love you honey."

"Love you too. Talk to you tomorrow, and see you in five days!"

She smiled. "Five days! Night babe."

"Night." He hung up.

She put the phone on the nightstand and snuggled down into the covers. *Five days*, she thought as she drifted off to sleep with Dug by her side, and Sally purring softly on her pillow.

3.

After he hung up the phone with Molly, Gary went about getting a shower. The hotel he was in was not as nice as some, but better than others. The bathroom was small, the kind you could just about shit, shower and shave in while standing in the same spot. That took its rating down a notch or two. But it was just for a night, and it seemed fairly clean.

He got out his UV wand and sanitized the bed before climbing in. He'd watched one of those specials about how dirty hotels were and was horrified. Molly had warned him not to watch it. She said what he didn't know wouldn't hurt him, but it was like a train wreck, and once he'd started watching it he couldn't stop. After that Gary had invested in a UV wand, and so had several of his friends when they were told about the horrors of the "organic substances" that could be found on a hotel comforter.

It took him forever to fall asleep, as it usually did when he was away from home. He missed his own bed. He missed feeling Dug at his feet. Most of all, though, he missed having Molly by his side. Even though Gary spent a lot of nights alone, he'd never gotten used to it.

He glanced at the clock and realized he only had a few hours left to get some sleep, and a long duty day ahead. So he redoubled his efforts and was soon dreaming about Molly.

He was back at home, standing at the front gate, looking at their house. It was a very cute little house. That is, cute as defined by Molly. She'd always wanted a house like this, and it suited the neighborhood they lived in. So, Gary had compromised with her. It wasn't something he would've picked out, but the inside of it was immaculate, just like he wanted. It was the perfect blend of the two of them.

The outside was a sunny yellow color with white trim. It had a porch in the front with a white banister, and white shutters surrounded the windows. It also had a white picket fence that circled the entire yard. Molly wanted Dug to have as much space as possible to run around in, and that yard did the trick.

Gary approached the house and went inside. He scanned the living room for Molly or Dug, but didn't find them. Dug always greeted Gary with such excitement when he came through the door – whether he'd been gone ten minutes or ten days. Where were they?

He crossed the dark hardwood floors to the kitchen and searched there. He found it just how he'd left it – dark granite countertops, cherry cabinetry, light stone floors, stainless steel appliances. But it seemed cold to him without Molly.

Gary went upstairs and rounded the corner, searching for his family. He padded softly to the master bedroom. Molly never closed the door when he was gone. She wanted the animals to be able to come and go as they pleased.

He found Molly curled up with Dug and Sally, indulging in an afternoon nap – one of his favorite things to do. It surprised him, because Molly didn't nap. She said she always woke up more tired than when she lay down. But he didn't question it in his dream. He simply slipped out of his pants and shirt and sidled up next to her.

She didn't wake all the way up, but she stirred and snuggled into Gary's chest as he spooned her. Dug didn't even raise his head, and of course Sally didn't acknowledge Gary at all.

He buried his face in Molly's hair and breathed in her glorious scent. His life was perfect. He had his dream job, flying to exotic locations, he had a dream wife, who was always there when he got home, and he had a dream house. What more could a guy want?

Gary dreamed about Molly all night long. He dreamed about taking her to The Pizza Garden. He dreamed about dropping in on her classes one day. He dreamed about cleaning up the fish tank.

When he woke up in the morning, he realized he'd spent the entire night with her, and smiled. Gary often wondered how normal couples felt, getting to spend every night together. He was gone six months of the year, so their nights together were precious.

He glanced at the clock and saw that it was only six-thirty. He opted not to text Molly yet, because he knew she wouldn't be up. She liked to sleep as long as possible, and was occasionally grouchy if woken up.

He got dressed and went downstairs to see what the hotel had to offer in the way of breakfast. It wasn't much: a bowl of apples and a variety of cereals – variety being a choice between Honey Nut Cheerios and Frosted Flakes – along with some hot coffee and run-of-the-mill creamers. It was enough, though. It was early, and Gary didn't often like to eat breakfast. He knew it might be awhile before he had the opportunity to eat lunch, so he swiped an extra apple for the road.

While he ate, CNN played on the closest TV.

"Scientists warn of an apocalyptic solar flare that could destroy life on Earth as we know it."

Gary choked on his cereal, laughing at the

sensationalism coming from the television so early in the morning. The media was really getting out of control. They'd lived through Y2K, and even survived the end of the Mayan calendar. Much to the dismay of some of the more radical Christians, the end wasn't in fact as near as the reporter would have them believe.

"Scientists say the flare could cause a catastrophic electromagnetic pulse that would shut down all electronics and electricity for anywhere between a few months and several years," the anchorwoman proclaimed.

Gary spied the remote on the next table and retrieved it. He changed the channel while the anchorwoman was speculating about the outright chaos that would follow such an event. It was too early for that kind of propaganda, if you asked him. Gary switched the TV to something a little more palatable at seven in the morning. SpongeBob SquarePants fit the bill. Gary chuckled at the cartoon as he finished off his cereal and prepared to face the day.

The Captain came in just as Gary was finishing up. "Oh, hey Clint," Gary said.

"Morning." Clint was a big man, tall and broad. He wasn't dressed for work yet, and wore sweatpants and a t-shirt down to breakfast. His brown hair was pointing in several directions, characteristic of him at that early hour.

They'd only had a handful of flights together, and in fact they would be parting ways again in Orlando. Clint was just finishing his seven-day stint, but Gary still had four days to go.

Clint didn't strike Gary as the friendliest fellow, and took a very minimalistic approach to conversation – limiting his responses to as few words as possible to get his point across, and only asking questions or initiating conversation when it was absolutely necessary.

They parted ways after breakfast to get cleaned up, and met in the lobby less than twenty minutes later. The walk out to the crew car was silent, and in fact, the entire ride over to the airport was quiet, save for the classical stylings of Philly's 101.7 FM. Luckily the airport was only a few miles away.

Really, Gary didn't mind Clint's quiet side. It was a hell of a lot better than some of the other yokels who talked non-stop while he was running checklists and trying to concentrate on charts. Given the choice, Gary would pick Clint any day. He was a hard worker and kept to himself. Really, Gary could do worse.

They stopped to get coffee and donuts for the passengers on the way, and then headed to the airplane to get set up.

The Hawker was a small business jet that seated nine people. Gary wasn't expecting that many people for this trip, but they could take them if they had to. Usually, they only had a handful of some of the wealthiest people in the country occupying the seats.

After cleaning up, running checks, and restocking the bird, they were ready for the passengers to arrive so they could get going.

Gary figured it was a good time to say good morning to Molly, so he sent her a text.

Morning beautiful! Can't wait to see ya in four days! Have a wonderful day!

She responded right away. *Morning handsome! Be safe today and can't wait to see you too!*

It was quickly followed by a picture of Dug with bedhead, and the caption: *Dug says good morning. Haha!*

Gary smiled. *Haha, morning Dug!* Gary typed. It was a classic picture, with Dug bleary-eyed, his hair going in every direction imaginable.

Clint walked up and nodded as he made eye contact. "Any word from the passengers?" Gary asked, locking his phone and jamming it back into his pocket.

"Nope."

"Well, I guess we wait."

Clint harrumphed at that. Flying wasn't really the

biggest part of the job, even though Gary thought it was the best part. The majority of the workday was spent waiting, a smaller percentage collecting whatever was requested, and an even smaller part actually flying.

So, they waited.

Darkness
4.

"Deep into that darkness peering, long I stood there, wondering, fearing, doubting, dreaming dreams no mortal ever dared to dream before."
– Edgar Allen Poe

Darkness is a funny thing. The mere absence of light brings uncertainty and fear – the breeding ground for chaos. It is so absolute. And yet, so easily defeated by a single flame, if only someone thinks to light a candle.

5.

The next morning Molly got up and went to class, prepared to hear the groans from her Modern Poetry class for their late papers. She usually punished them with half a letter grade for every class they were late, but she wasn't sure what to do to compensate for her own lateness. She thought if she could come up with a few options, like having class in the garden one day or letting them pick the next poem to discuss, and let them choose, they'd be happy.

Her other classes held better prospects. She was excited because the day brought discussions about *Gulliver's Travels* in British Literature, and *The Poisonwood Bible* in Modern Fiction. Save for the groaning from Modern Poetry, she expected it to be a pretty good day.

It happened in the middle of Modern Fiction. A student had asked what point Kingsolver was trying to make by sacrificing the family's youngest child.

"What could possibly be worth killing such an innocent character?" she asked.

"Well, what do you think? Do you think the father is so taken by his 'mission' to 'save' the heathens in the Congo that his youngest is a fair sacrifice, as you put it?

What's one life if it saves a handful of others?" Molly had just said it to spur the discussion. She often made extreme statements in class just to stir the pot and get a good discussion going.

She sat cross-legged on top of her desk looking at the rows of students as hands shot into the air. She smiled and surveyed their faces. Their expressions ranged from angry to mischievous. Molly picked one that seemed undecided. "Mia, what do you think?"

Before she could answer, the lights went out. It wasn't really all that dark, because the back wall had several windows on it, and for that she was thankful.

"Um…OK. Just a second here, let me poke my head into the hall and see if I can find out what the deal is," Molly said as she got down off the desk.

The students whispered to each other as she walked to the door. "Settle down. I'm sure it's just a power surge, and it'll be back on before I can even find out what happened."

"My phone doesn't work. Does yours?" A boy in the front row asked his neighbor.

It caught Molly's attention. "Is your battery dead?" she asked.

"No. I left home with a full charge."

Other students began retrieving their phones. The consensus was unanimous. No one's phone worked. Molly took her phone out of her pocket to see, and to her surprise, it displayed nothing but a black screen.

She frowned and continued on her journey to the door. "I'll find out what's going on. Just stay calm," Molly assured them. They all looked worried.

Teachers were beginning to poke their heads out of their doors, making similar inquiries about the outage. No one seemed to know what was going on. Normally, there would be an announcement or some sort of directive about what to do, but they'd never encountered this type of outage before.

Molly ran to her office to grab her laptop and returned to the classroom. By then the kids were getting a little panicky, letting their imaginations run away with them.

"Why would the power *and* our phones be out? What could possibly cause something like that?"

"How long do you think it'll be out?"

"My mom said she thinks the apocalypse is coming. She said the signs are all there."

Another student burst out laughing. "Your mom is crazy."

Molly interrupted before a fight could break out. "OK, enough. The power will probably be back on soon. The school has an emergency generator that should kick in any minute now. Just let me get my laptop going, and I'll see if I can get some information about it."

"Dr. Bonham, if the power's out, will you be able to get online?"

By then, Molly had already gotten her computer out and was trying to get it powered up. "Oh, that's a good point. Probably not."

Then she noticed nothing was happening with her computer. She held the power button down, with no response. She waited a few moments and tried again. Still nothing.

"What on Earth…" Molly muttered.

"What's wrong?"

"Um…I'm not sure. I can't get my computer to come on."

"What should we do? Can we go home?"

"I don't know about that either. The stairwells are dark, I don't want there to be a stampede. Just give me a minute to think about the options."

They weren't prepared for something like this. They knew exactly what to do for a tornado, a fire alarm, or an earthquake. But this was new territory.

There really was no reason not to continue with class. The only things they were using were the lights, and it was plenty bright enough to continue the discussion without them. However, the kids were rattled, and quite frankly so was Molly. Continuing with the discussion seemed fruitless, but leaving right this second wasn't a good option either. She didn't want to put the students in an unsafe situation.

"Let me run back to the department head's office and see what he thinks. You guys wait here until I get back, OK?" Molly looked at them all, seeing the panic starting to bubble up. "I mean it," she said sternly. She thought giving them a task, even if it was just sitting still, would help occupy their minds.

Molly caught up with Terry Longman in the hallway. She looked at him and shrugged. "Now what?" she asked.

His normally disheveled appearance looked a little more unruly in his stress. His grey hair stood straight out and his tweed coat hung unevenly. "I have no idea. I'm telling the kids and teachers to stay put for now. There are no lights in the stairwells, and I don't want anyone getting trampled. Let's wait twenty minutes or so and see if it comes back. If it doesn't, we'll let the classes go one room at a time to prevent a stampede. So, since your class is at the far end of the building, they may be here a while."

"No problem. Just keep me posted."

Molly stopped in Cindy's room, knowing she had a rowdy group this time of day. They were arguing with her about getting to leave.

"HEY!" Molly hollered to get their attention. They were immediately quiet. "This is a professional environment, not a middle school. Arguing is not tolerated. You will stay put until Dr. Longman says you can go. He's making his rounds now, and he's said if power is not restored in another twenty minutes or so, he will let everyone go home. However, he doesn't want any misconduct, so he'll be letting classes go one room at a time. Just sit tight."

A unified groan went up. "Hey, you're supposed to be

in this class right now anyway! I don't want to hear your complaints," Molly said.

"Yeah, well I'm not sitting here any longer than I have to. Class gets out at three, and I'm out of here at three," declared an older student, dressed in black jeans and a black t-shirt. It was obvious that his silver chains, piercings, and long hair were meant to intimidate. Molly was unfazed.

"You'll do whatever the head of the department says you'll do. No questions about it. This is considered an emergency situation, and for your own safety and the safety of others, you'll stay put for now. We're not keeping you here forever, so just relax."

Cindy had that deer-in-headlights look. Molly turned and put her hand on Cindy's upper arm. "Hey, straighten up. These kids'll eat you alive if you let them. Don't. Terry said he'll be letting classes go one at a time if the power's not back in twenty minutes. The process shouldn't take too long, since there's about ten rooms downstairs and ten up here, so just hold the fort for maybe an hour tops, OK?"

She nodded her head. "OK," Molly said. She squeezed Cindy's arm for reassurance.

Molly went back into the hall to face her own class. They were buzzing with the possibilities of what such an outage could mean, but they were not nearly as troublesome as Cindy's group.

"Alright," Molly said, getting their attention. "Dr. Longman is giving it about twenty minutes to come back. If it doesn't, he's going to let you guys go, but one classroom at a time. Since we're on the far end of the building we might be waiting for a bit. So sit tight."

A collective sigh rang out. "So, what do you want to do? Would you like to continue our discussion or just talk among yourselves?" Molly asked.

"I want to know what's happening." Several voices sprang up in agreement.

"Well, yeah. So do I. But I'm not omniscient, so I can't help you there. I couldn't even begin to speculate what could cause the power to go out, as well as zap your phones, and seemingly my lap top – which I'm none too pleased about, by the way."

"Why? Don't you think it'll come back?" The student who asked sounded frightened.

"Oh, well yeah, it'll come back. I'm just hoping the surge didn't fry anything. I mean, if nothing else, I'll get a brand new computer, but there were a few things I hadn't had time to back up yet, so I'll be a little peeved if that's how it plays out."

"Do you think our phones will come back?"

"Well, I don't know. I imagine since it's such a widespread issue at the minimum the phone companies might provide you with replacements. Might bankrupt them though. Who knows. It's hard to speculate without knowing the cause of it."

One student in the middle of the classroom piped up. "I saw on CNN this morning a thing about a catastrophic solar flare. I bet it happened. And I'll bet the power doesn't come back on in twenty minutes, or twenty days."

The words "twenty days" echoed around the room, weighing heavily on the occupants.

Molly cleared her throat. "Now, now, they're always saying sensational things like that on TV. I'm sure it's not that serious." She made eye contact with one of the more panic-stricken students. "Everything will be fine."

The discussion went on like that for the next hour and a half. One student proposed that it was a terrorist attack, that someone had sent out a signal that disabled all electronic devices, but that didn't really explain why the lights went out. Another student thought the surge was so dramatic that it disabled nearby electronics. But other students debunked that theory, saying they would've heard or felt something if that was the case.

Just then, Terry poked his head in. "Dr. Longman.

What's the good word?" Molly asked.

"You guys can go now, but I want a slow and orderly departure, OK? One girl already fell on the stairs and may have hurt her ankle pretty bad. We're still trying to figure out how to get help here. So get yourselves home safely, OK?"

One student brought up something Molly hadn't thought of. "Dr. Longman? What about tomorrow?"

"What do you mean?"

"What do we do if the power's still out?"

"It won't be," he said firmly.

After all the kids cleared out, Molly went to her office to try and call Gary from the landline, but the phone wouldn't come on. It was a cordless with an answering machine that she had bought herself. She couldn't remember what kind of phone Cindy had in her office; if it was one the school had issued, or one she'd brought in. Molly decided to take a chance and see if Cindy was there. Of course, she wasn't. Molly walked to Cindy's room and it was empty as well. Molly was surprised Cindy had left without saying anything, but shrugged it off. She'd seemed upset and probably wanted to know how her family was.

Terry's office turned out to be a bust as well. In fact, no one was left in the building. It was creepy to be in there alone with all the lights off, so she decided to just go home. Maybe the power was on there. And if it wasn't, she wanted to get there before dark so she could get the candles out.

Molly walked to her scooter, feeling distracted. There were people everywhere. The entire school had emptied all at once, which was very unusual. Different classes scheduled at different times generally made it so no one had to fight to leave. But as Molly looked around, she noticed no one was leaving. The parking lot was silent, save for people talking to each other. Not a single engine was running.

Molly got her helmet out from under the seat and fastened the strap while she observed the crowd. They seemed to be engrossed in solving their own problems, not realizing that everyone around them was experiencing the same thing. It never occurred to her that she was about to join their plight.

She tried to turn the scooter on, and nothing happened.

That's odd, Molly thought.

She tried it again with no luck. *Of course Gary is still gone, so it's me to my own rescue once again.*

She looked around and felt bad for some of the others. Especially Cindy, who was nowhere to be seen. She could just walk home. It was only a few miles. But Cindy lived a long way from here. Molly wondered what Cindy was going to do. She looked for Cindy's car one more time, and didn't see it.

Maybe she got lucky and didn't have any trouble, she thought.

As she walked her scooter to the edge of the lot, she spotted Cindy. She was more than frazzled. Molly pushed her scooter over, still donning her helmet.

"Hey!" Molly called. "You OK?"

"Not really! My car won't start, and my phone doesn't work so I can't even call Tom. I have no idea if the kids are OK or where they are."

"OK, let's think about this rationally. It's two-thirty in the afternoon. They're probably all at school. Tom is at work. Just formulate a game plan and you'll feel better, less out of control. Do you want to go home and see if anyone is there first, or do you want to go to the kids' school?" Once it was out of her mouth she regretted it. Molly hadn't really said she would go with Cindy, but it was implied. She knew it would be after dark by the time she could get home if she ran all over town. But if they started at the kids' school, that wasn't that far, and maybe she could get a ride home from there.

"Yeah, but how will we get to the school?" Cindy tightly gripped the steering wheel on her SUV, already buckled in and ready to rush to her family. However, she was going nowhere fast.

"We'll have to walk."

They kept up a brisk pace, and it took under an hour to cross the two and a half miles. Luckily, all three kids went to the same school, so at least they didn't have to walk all over kingdom come to collect them individually.

The power was out at the school too, and it was controlled chaos. The sprawling building resembled an anthill, with kids moving sporadically all over the campus.

They approached the frazzled teachers one at a time, who took note of the children's mother picking them up. Cindy asked them to let Tom know if he popped by. There were still a huge number of kids milling around, which surprised Molly. But, really, if everyone was having the same car trouble that people on campus were having, it'd probably be a while before all the kids were picked up. Molly couldn't help but wonder what would happen to the kids whose parents worked outside the city. But then again, those people probably weren't affected by the outage. They probably didn't even know what was going on.

Once all three kids were collected, Molly asked, "OK, now what?" Cindy's house was another two miles away, but it was in the opposite direction of Molly's, putting her about six miles from home. It was a long way to walk as the daylight waned.

Suddenly, Molly's situation dawned on Cindy. "Molly, why don't you head home? I can get the kids home from here. Tom will probably meet us there."

The offer was tempting. Molly looked at the three kids, the five-year-old in particular. Two miles was a long way to ask a kid that age to walk. "What about Melody? She's too little to walk that far."

"I'll carry her when she gets tired. Don't worry. We'll

be fine. It'll be too dark for you to walk home if you come with us."

And then what would I do about poor Dug and Sally? Molly thought. She weighed the options, looking guiltily at Cindy. "Really, Molly. Go. We'll be fine. It'll just be good to be home and all together. Probably by the time we get there, the power will be back on!"

She was absolutely right. Molly sighed. "OK." She reached out and grabbed Cindy's shoulders, looking straight into her eyes. "I'll see you tomorrow." It wasn't a question. It was a statement. Despite her assurance, a small part of Molly felt like it might be a while before they saw each other again.

"Sounds great. Hopefully, everything'll be back to normal by then."

"Everything *will* be back to normal by then," Molly said, and walked away, leaving her dear friend to care for her family while Molly went to care for hers.

Molly had to make her way back to the college to get her scooter. It took over an hour to push the scooter home, but it was a nice day so she wasn't bothered too much. She *was* bothered by the fact that she wasn't passed by any cars at all the entire time. There were cars parked on the side of the road, as usual for the historic town, but there was no one driving on the street. In fact, cars were stopped in the street, abandoned. But no one was irritated. No one was honking at the obstruction. No one was trying to get through. Everything had come to an abrupt halt, and left nothing but stillness and silence in its wake. It made her anxious and jittery. Walking with Cindy had provided a bit of a distraction. Alone it seemed too quiet, too still, too...unnatural.

Molly couldn't get her scooter into the garage because the door wouldn't go up. It seemed the power was out here, too. She sighed, parked the scooter in front of the garage, and went to the front door.

Dug was his regular energetic self, but the house was

quiet without the hum of the refrigerator, the air conditioning, or any of the other appliances that collectively made up the soundtrack of her home.

She busied herself looking for candles and matches and placing them in strategic places all over the house – the kitchen, the bathrooms, the bedroom. Once she was done, though, she didn't know what else to do.

Molly checked her cell phone periodically, but still wasn't having any luck.

It was nearly dark, and she'd really thought the power would be back on by now. She wasn't really hungry, but felt she should eat something lest it spoil. She got out the gas burner they used during hurricanes and for camping and warmed up some leftovers. She dreaded the thought of a cold shower, and silently prayed that there was some warm water left from before the power went out. The lukewarm shower was the warmest she would get for a long time.

That night she didn't get to speak to Gary. Landlines had pretty much gone the way of the dodo a few years back, so he had no other way to get in touch, save for e-mail, and of course that was out too. It was the first time she'd gone to bed knowing she wouldn't get to speak to him since they started dating. They'd talked every day in some way, shape, or fashion since before they were married. Molly hoped he wasn't too worried.

Molly put off going to bed as long as possible. She didn't want to sleep with a candle lit because she was afraid it would start a fire, but it was so dark. There wasn't even the glow of streetlights for comfort. There was no hum of appliances, no noise from the air conditioning, no light from anywhere, except the half-moon, which really wasn't all that bright.

She didn't even know what time it was for sure. Her watch had quit right around the time the power went out. All she knew was that it was sometime after dark.

Sally and Dug followed her everywhere, and when

Molly went up to go to bed they both followed her, which surprised her. Even Sally settled down next to Molly that night. It was a small comfort knowing they were both at least within reach if something happened. She didn't know what she was expecting, but she just felt unsettled.

The darkness was so...penetrating. She couldn't wait for morning, when the world would be returned to the light.

6.

Gary played Texas hold 'em on his cell phone while they waited in the airport. Clint was watching CNN and Gary halfheartedly listened. Clint had free reign on the remote. They were the only two schmucks still waiting on passengers.

The Fixed Based Operation was fairly nice, at least. Some FBO's were really a hole. Nothing more than a trailer on the side of the ramp, and they were expected to rendezvous with their high-end clients there? This one had leather couches in the lounge; a big, high-quality TV for entertainment; free hot coffee; and well-stocked vending machines.

Suddenly Gary's phone turned off. He looked up and noticed the lights were out in the lounge and the TV was silent. The power was out. He tried to switch his phone back on but it didn't respond.

"Hey, Clint, is your phone working?"

He took his phone from his pocket and frowned. "No."

Gary walked to the desk to see if they knew what was going on. The woman behind the desk spoke to someone behind her. "I can't get a dial tone. Can you? …Huh.

What the heck?" Then she noticed Gary standing there. "How can I help you?"

"I don't really know. Do you know what's going on? Is there anything we can do?"

"I don't know, on both accounts. Sit tight. You've got a full tank of gas, so if your passengers get here, I see no reason why you can't just go, as long as you can talk to the tower."

"Well, I wasn't worried about that. Our phones aren't working, and I guess yours aren't either, so I guess we won't be hearing from our passengers any time soon. Do you have a rotary phone, or something that doesn't plug into an outlet, that might work?"

"Oh, uh…" She thought for a moment. "No, I don't think we do."

"No problem. I'm sure everything will be back online before too long."

Gary walked back to Clint and shook his head. Clint had heard the whole conversation, and didn't like it one bit. "I'm gonna go check the airplane." He walked out without waiting for a response.

Gary decided to wait in the lounge in case their passengers showed up.

The sound of an explosion shook the windows and rattled his chest. Gary immediately ran out to the Hawker.

Clint popped his head out. "What the hell was that?"

"I thought you might know."

The fog hanging low in the distance made it difficult to see. They walked to the edge of the ramp together and scanned the horizon. Gary thought he could make out an unnatural orange light to the west.

"Looks like something funny at the end of 9 Right."

Gary squinted towards the glow. "Where are the emergency vehicles? If it was a crash, shouldn't they be responding?"

"Mmm." Clint scrutinized the airport. They both strained for the sound of rescue that always followed a crash. The distinctive sound of sirens was noticeably absent. The silence they left was crushing.

Gary shook his head. "It must not have been a crash. That's the only explanation." He paused. "Do you think we should go check it out?"

"No. By the time we got over there, we'd only be in the way. It's quite a hike to that side of the airport, even if we took one of the golf carts. They'll be fine. There're people on site whose job it is to help with that stuff." Gary nodded and Clint cleared his throat. "Anyway, we've got a problem of our own to deal with."

They both turned to walk back to the Hawker. "What's wrong?"

"Nothing works. Damn thing won't respond to anything. It's a giant six-million-dollar paperweight."

That's odd, Gary thought. Ten minutes ago they had finished all their checks and were ready and waiting to go. Nothing had indicated a problem then. *What the hell is going on here?*

Gary walked to the airplane to see for himself. Even though Clint wasn't the exaggerating type, Gary couldn't believe the situation had changed so dramatically so quickly. Yet, the sound of the explosion still echoed in his mind.

He climbed the Hawker's steps and sat down in the right seat. Everything was dark in the cockpit. He tried to power on the engines and the control panel. Nothing. Even the tablet for their charts wouldn't turn on. The cabin lights, the entertainment system, all nothing.

After flipping every switch multiple times with no response, Gary sat back in the right seat and sighed. Clint was right. It was a giant paperweight.

Clint grunted when they made eye contact with the same conclusion – something was seriously wrong here.

It's not related to the explosion. Our problem is isolated. Unrelated to the power outage. So was the explosion. Must be a bizarre series of incidents, nothing more, Gary tried to convince himself. It didn't add up, though. It was too coincidental. But why would a power outage cause a plane to crash? *But...if their instruments all went dark like ours did while they were on short final in the fog...* He shook his head to clear the ominous thoughts. He still wasn't totally convinced it was a plane crash. *Was there a fuel station at the end of 9 Right? Even so, wouldn't that also require at least a fire truck? Was the Sheriff's Department doing a demonstration today? That would need a fire truck too, but maybe not the sirens...*

He ran through the possibilities as they walked back to the lounge and went straight to the desk. "Hey, we're going to need someone from maintenance out here right away," Clint said.

Gary looked at him, confused. *Oh, right, our own problems.* He was having trouble focusing.

The woman behind the desk was frazzled, and the two pilots hanging around her FBO weren't her top priority. "I'm sorry, but the phones still aren't working. I can't get someone out here right now. Can you wait until we can get this figured out?"

Clint and Gary looked at each other skeptically. "Not really. We don't have any way to get in touch with our passengers, and if they show up without a working airplane, they're going to be pissed."

"I don't know what to tell you," she said. She was sympathetic, but she had bigger issues to deal with.

Gary looked at Clint. "OK, I'm going over to maintenance. You stay here in case the passengers get here."

"That's fine by me."

Gary turned back to the girl behind the desk. "Lemme have the keys to the rental we just returned. I'll just be a second."

"Sure," she said and absently and handed them over. Luckily, a representative hadn't come to pick the car up yet. But his luck ran out as he approached the base-model Chevy. The remote keyless entry didn't work, so he put the key in the lock to get in. It opened the driver's door, but not any of the others when he turned it again.

When he tried to start the car, nothing happened. It was absolute silence. No sound from the starter, no response from the radio. Nothing. He turned everything off, the air conditioning, the radio, any interior lights that may have been on, and tried again. Nothing. Gary was getting annoyed.

He sat in the driver's seat and thought for a minute. He glanced at the car next to him, and thought something looked...off. He couldn't quite figure it out. It wasn't on, so nothing would be illuminated- except. Except a light that should have been on, wasn't. Most cars had a blinking light on the dashboard, to let them know their basic security system worked. It blinked all the time. So either the security system wasn't working in that car, or nothing was. He leaned forward and looked at the light in his own car. It was dark. He got out and walked to the next car; its light was also out.

Gary walked back into the building with a sense of foreboding. He didn't have a firm grasp on what was going on, but the more he discovered, the worse the situation seemed. He couldn't help but circle his thoughts back to the explosion. *If the car won't start, is it possible emergency vehicles couldn't respond to whatever happened?* It was a frightening thought. *How could that be? What on Earth would knock out everything?* Something pulled at the edge of his mind, but he couldn't quite put the pieces together. There were just too many of them, and more being added all the time.

He approached Clint. "The car isn't working. I'll have to walk. I'll be back as soon as I can."

"K," he said. Clint's dark expression mirrored Gary's thoughts on the situation.

The maintenance hangar was a long way from the FBO where they routinely met their passengers. The FBO was made to meet all of their creature comforts, while the maintenance hangar was set back and out of the way, so the wealthy clientele wouldn't be exposed to the grime and noise.

It took what Gary assumed was around a half hour to walk the distance. He couldn't say for sure as his watch had quit. The fog was lifting by that time, and he looked out across the ramp to find planes backed up in a scene of chaos such as he had never witnessed. It was almost like they couldn't communicate. No one was moving, and he noticed their beacons weren't on. Four airliners were stacked in a row on the taxiway without beacons flashing. *That's really odd*, he thought. He stood and watched the scene for a moment, thinking he would see its resolution, but after a few moments he had to move on.

I have my own problems, Gary reminded himself. *But if that doesn't clear up, how are we going to get out, even if our airplane does start up?* He sighed. *One thing at a time.*

The hangar was dark, but there was a flurry of activity. Apparently the power was out on that end of the airport too.

Gary found the guy in charge without too much trouble. He reached out and touched his arm, and the man turned to face him. "Hey, I've got a big problem."

He could tell by the uniform that Gary was a pilot, and just shook his head. "Yeah, tell me about it. Nothing works. All of the avionics and everything in all these babies died at once." He gestured to the three jets parked in the hanger.

Gary was baffled. "Are you kidding me?"

"Nope. You're going to have to get in line with your problems, kid. Sorry."

"Well, when you have time, I'm at MCC's FBO. Just send someone over, would ya?"

He looked skeptically at Gary, and sighed. "I'll see what I can do."

Gary turned to leave, but then turned back. "Do you happen to have a rotary phone?"

"No, we don't. And I kind of wish we did. We can't make any calls."

Gary nodded, thanked him, and left. He walked back to MCC, hoping the situation would improve during his trudge across the airport. He noticed people using the slides to get off stranded airplanes right in the middle of the runway. They gathered in the grass, not knowing what to do.

Then he noticed the smoke. Thick, black smoke that could only mean death, and lots of it, was rising from the end of 9 Right. Gary frowned and picked up his pace.

Unfortunately, when he got back to MCC, the situation hadn't changed. Clint was still the only one waiting in the lounge, but the women behind the desk seemed to be getting a little more panicky.

When they saw Gary, relief shone in their eyes. "Are they coming? Do they have power down there?"

"Actually, no they don't. And the scene out there is kind of a CF. They're abandoning the aircrafts – using the slides to get off and congregating in the grass. No one is taking off, and they're having a hell of a time clearing the taxiways." He paused. "And there's smoke coming from the end of 9 Right. Something major is going on here. I just don't know what."

Clint had crept up next to Gary while he was relaying information, and startled him a little. "What can we do?" he asked.

They were both men of action, not ones to sit around and wait for someone else to solve their problems. However, Gary had no answer. He had no idea what to do. He'd gained more pieces on the trek out to maintenance, but none of them seemed to fit together. Walking to the scene of the explosion would only endanger them and wasn't a good option. There was nothing that could be done for them, whatever had happened. All Gary and Clint could do was wait.

After a while, they both started to get hungry. The power still wasn't on, and they couldn't leave or use the phone to order food. They couldn't even use the vending machines. All that delicious junk food stared at Gary through the glass.

"Do you have a key for this machine?" he asked the girl behind the desk.

"I'm not sure. Let me check."

"I'll leave money if you can get it open."

She nodded and disappeared to a place where they apparently kept keys for the machines. She reappeared a few moments later with a key ring in hand. "Here we are. You boys hungry?"

"Yeah, I am." Gary looked over at Clint and he nodded. "This might be the best we can do for now, Clint." Vending-machine food wouldn't hold them over for long, but he didn't think they'd have to live off it. He was sure this would be resolved soon and they'd be out of there.

Gary chose a bag of mini peanut butter cracker sandwiches. He figured at least he'd get some protein that way. He gave the girl a dollar and grabbed a cup of water from the cooler. It was actually still pretty cold. He estimated it'd been a few hours, but couldn't be sure. It seemed like a long time when they were just sitting.

He sat on the couch with his feet on the coffee table and dug into the crackers. Gary started thinking about Molly. He wondered what she was doing, and if the same thing was going on there. It had to be an isolated incident. He was sure if they went to the next town the power would be on, and they could get a hot meal. Maybe they could even get some help. No, they were probably already sending help.

Molly would be worried if Gary didn't get in touch. She was expecting them to be on the ground in Orlando soon. Gary frowned. He didn't know what to do about that. He couldn't text her. He couldn't call her. He couldn't email her. He couldn't get in touch with her in any way. He started to panic a little. The isolation was overwhelming. His breathing quickened, and he began to sweat.

Clint noticed. "What's wrong?"

"I just realized I can't get in touch with Molly. I've never been in this situation before. I've always had some way to get in touch with her, and know she was OK."

"Hey, it's fine. Any minute now things'll be back to normal. No need to panic." He said it with such an even tone, Gary believed him.

"Yeah, I'm sure you're right. Nothing to worry about, huh?"

He nodded his agreement, relaxed against the plush leather couch, and returned to daydreaming about Molly. *Late afternoon, so she'll probably be wrapping up her last class of the day. How long will she stay at school today? Will she have dinner with Cindy again? What's Dug up to?* He smiled at the thought of Dug. He was such a great dog – so happy and grateful. Gary missed him then, and hoped he'd get to go home soon, especially after a day like today. If nothing else, he'd be home in a few days, and then he'd be off for an entire week. He couldn't wait to be back with his family.

That got him wondering. *If we do make it to Orlando eventually, will they give us the rest of the week off, due to the stress?* He shook his head. *Probably not.* It was just confusing, not terribly traumatic. Their little corner of the airport was fairly sheltered. They were just waiting, which is probably what they would've been doing if the power was on. There was no guarantee the passengers would have arrived yet, so they could very well be sitting here, power or not.

The day crept on, and Gary watched the people stream back into the main terminals. For whatever reason, no one came their way. They probably decided it was best for everyone out on the runways to stay together. Gary wrinkled his nose, glad they were spared being treated like cattle by the authorities at PHL.

As the sun started to go down, worry stole back into Gary's thoughts. He turned to Clint. "Whaddya think?"

"I expect we should stay here."

"OK, but all night? We can't sleep here."

"Why not? Where do you plan to go, and how do you plan to get there?"

It was a good question. And he was right. Why couldn't they spend the night at MCC? The girls didn't know what to do. They didn't want to leave the FBO unmanned, but they had families, and didn't live that far from the airport. They wanted to walk home, and Gary couldn't blame them. If he had the chance to be with family tonight, he would've taken it.

"OK, why don't you girls go home, and Clint and I will lock up and sleep here tonight. We've got food, water, couches and a bathroom. Everything we need. I'm sure the power will come back on by the morning. We'll give the keys to whoever shows up first."

Everyone knew the crew that was supposed to relieve them wasn't coming. MCC was open twenty-four hours, but with this outage they couldn't be expected to operate normally. At any rate, if someone showed up and needed something, the boys would be there.

"Perfect," one of the girls said with relief in her eyes. "Let me dig out the flashlights for you boys so it doesn't get too dark in here."

"Thanks again for doing this," another girl said as she handed Gary a giant silver flashlight. He tried to switch it on, but didn't have any luck. He frowned at her.

"Maybe the lantern will work?" she asked, hanging on to a small bit of hope.

Gary raised an eyebrow and turned his attention to a large camping-style lantern. It was battery-powered too, so he didn't hold his breath as he flipped the switch. Nothing happened.

Panic crept into their voices. "We don't have anything

else. It's not like we keep candles around."

Gary shook his head. "No, why would you? These would be enough in a hurricane or outage situation." He turned to them. "Listen, we'll be fine. It's just a little dark. We're big boys. Go home before it gets too dark to find your way, OK?"

"OK," they both said at once, relief and guilt fighting for time on their faces.

They planned to walk to the home of the one who lived the closest; they'd separate from there.

When Gary locked the door behind them, the sound of the bolt slamming home resonated. Their band of refugees, as it were, had just shrunk by half.

Clint could see his despair. "I found a deck of cards when we were looking for candles and supplies. Wanna play?"

Heck, there wasn't anything else to do. "Sure."

So they played cards. They pulled the table close to the window where the moonlight was shining in the brightest. Clint taught Gary how to play all kinds of games – poker games he hadn't played before, although Gary didn't think those were very fun with just two people, something called 'down and up', euchre, and some Gary didn't remember the name of. He felt it was a relief to have something to keep his mind off the status quo, and almost have some normalcy, even if they were playing by moonlight. He almost felt like it was fun.

Gary was quite certain more than once that Clint tried to cheat and say his card was an ace when it was really a deuce. It was hard telling sometimes in the darkness, and made for some lively games.

They played for a long time, and Gary thought it was pretty late when they finally decided to try and get some sleep. They chose couches and settled in. They got blankets from the plane and used the throw pillows on the couches. It was no five-star resort hotel, but they were warm, dry and safe. It was the last time he would enjoy such luxuries for a long time.

Gary listened to Clint's even breathing and wondered about Molly. He knew she would be worried after not hearing from him all day, and he was concerned about her. He hoped she could get some sleep tonight, and he prayed that she would know he was safe.

He drifted off to sleep thinking the same thing he did every night he was away. *I love you, Molly, and I can't wait to hold you in my arms again.*

Speculation
7.

"Time destroys the speculation of men, but it confirms nature."
— Marcus Tullius Cicero

Confusion rode in on the coattails of darkness. Everyone in the world thought normalcy would be restored any minute, and no one was thinking in terms of permanency – not yet at least.

Communication was taken back to the times before Alexander Graham Bell, before Morse code, before the Pony Express. There was no one to talk to except the neighbors. The world shrank to walking distance. No longer was there news of other countries, other cities, or other places. In fact, no longer was there news at all.

Each community assumed they were the only ones stricken with the debilitating problem, and that soon their neighboring cities would come to their aid.

They were wrong.

8.

After about two days, Molly really started to worry. None of her neighbors knew anything. There was no word. Nothing. No communication from emergency relief teams. No inkling that help was on the way.

Water was becoming a problem. She didn't realize it that first night when she settled in with Dug and Sally, but the water had stopped, leaving a lot of people in a pretty desperate state. It seemed odd to Molly that the water and power were out at the same time, with no natural disaster to blame...unless the power was out at the actual pumping stations.

She had quite a bit of bottled water on hand, but nothing to flush the toilet with. She walked to the beach and got a bucket of sea water for flushing and some for bathing. Clearly, bathing was about to become a luxury. There was a stream of fresh water a little further away, in the opposite direction of the beach, and she thought she might have to resort to using that for washing and flushing if this went on too long. Molly didn't know what she would do if her supply of drinking water ran out. *I could boil water over the grill, but what will I do when the charcoal runs out?* she wondered. *Gather wood. I would gather wood.*

She started to realize there seemed to be practical answers for most of her questions. But there were some big ones she had nothing for. *What happened to Gary? Where is he? Is he all right? Will he still come home in a few days? Or is the power out where he's at as well? What if he was in the air when everything went out?* She tried to push the thoughts from her mind and focus on more immediate problems.

Those first days, Molly tried to eat what she could in the refrigerator and the freezer, but inevitably some of it spoiled. She even fed some of the meat to Dug and Sally, and they thought they were in paradise. She ended up throwing some of it away though, and as she was cleaning out the fridge, she wondered when they would come to take the trash.

It seemed like everything had come to a screeching halt. There had been no work, no community services, and no news for the past two days. Several times a day, the neighbors gathered in the street to talk about what they thought was going on. Some said they thought this was happening in more places than just their town. Otherwise, there would have been help, or at least contact from the outside world.

The thought filled Molly with a sense of dread. *If the Blackout was more widespread, we may have to learn to live like this for an extended period. Maybe even a few weeks,* she thought. Luckily, their area was used to being without power due to the hurricanes that regularly pummeled the area, so most of the neighborhood wasn't without food or basic supplies. However, no one had enough to last over a week. Well, almost no one.

Jimmy Jean was a nut. At least everyone in the neighborhood thought so. A retired military man, he was one of those extremists, telling anyone who would listen what would happen during a catastrophic event. He was convinced a government collapse was inevitable; the only question was when. He had enough food stores in his basement to last for months, and had even given Molly and Gary a tour once, trying to educate them on the importance of preparedness. Gary had been annoyed, but Molly thought he was sweet and harmless. Jimmy's wife had died years before he'd moved to the area, and they'd never had kids. Molly decided the "end is near" stuff was sort of a hobby for him, something to occupy his time. Nothing more than that.

Now that she was surrounded by darkness, Molly wondered what he thought about all this. He'd been noticeably absent at the neighborhood gossip fests, which wasn't like him. He always liked to spread his apocalyptic views, and what better time than now?

Molly decided to walk over there and find out if he was OK. He lived a few streets over, near the outskirts of town. That day, it was warm for early October, and Molly broke into a sweat before she arrived at Jimmy's door.

She knocked and waited patiently for a reply. There were no sounds inside, no one stirring, no one moving to answer her knocks. She knocked again. "Hey, Jimmy? It's Molly! You OK?"

No answer. Molly walked around the back of the house, trying to see in a few of the windows. She was too short for most, but the basement windows weren't a problem. She laid down on the ground and peered in. It was dark in there, but she could make out Jimmy's shelves of supplies, and thought she caught movement in the shadows, but couldn't be sure.

"Jimmy?" she said a little louder. "Hey! Are you OK?"

She sat up in the grass near the window well, trying to decide what to do. If he was hurt in there, she should try to help him. But if he was just out he'd be mad if she broke a window.

A clicking noise behind her interrupted her thoughts. "Whaddya want?"

Her relief was short-lived. She turned around to find a shotgun pointed at her face, with Jimmy on the other end.

"Jesus Jimmy! What the hell?" She brushed the barrel of the gun away from her face, but he quickly repositioned it.

"I'm not gonna ask ya again." His voice was low. She'd never seen him like this before. He might have been a little nutty, but Molly never thought he was dangerous.

"I just came to see if you were OK. I haven't seen you in a few days, and it seemed like what was going on was your bread and butter, so I got worried. Sue me."

He lowered the gun. "Oh. I thought ya might be here for my food."

She eyed him. "Seriously, Jimmy? It's been two days."

He cleared his throat as he disarmed the weapon. "Well, as ya can see, I'm fine. So you can go back home."

"If that's what you want." She'd never seen him acting so prickly before, except towards people who laughed at his theories. She wasn't laughing. "Jimmy, what's wrong? What's going on?"

"Can't you see, Molly? It's happened!" His eyes had a feral quality about them that Molly didn't care for. "As soon as everyone realizes that, it'll be every man for himself. And I'll tell you one thing, those sorry sons of bitches aren't getting one thing from me. I warned you, didn't I?"

She sighed. "Yes. Yes you did." She paused. "You don't think the power'll come back soon?" She had no reason to believe otherwise. But clearly, Jimmy did.

"No, honey. I don't."

"State your sources." It was a phrase she often used with Jimmy when they debated about his theories.

"It's too much to recover from just like that, Molly. The water's off, the phones are out, all communications have been severed, transportation has been brought to a screeching halt." He paused and shook his head. "What they're saying on the radio doesn't give me a warm fuzzy either. If it was just one of those things, we might expect a speedy recovery, but it's too much. We're gonna be in the dark for a long time."

"Wait, your radio works?"

"Of course it does. Kept it in my filing cabinet for just such an emergency. "

Molly wasn't following.

"It's a makeshift Faraday cage, Molly." Molly looked at him blankly. "You know, to protect it from EMPs?"

"Right. Remind me what an EMP is."

He rolled his eyes. "Don't you ever listen to me? An electro-magnetic pulse. it knocks the power out. Who knows what caused it, but the result it pretty clear."

She shook her head. "Back to the point, Jimmy. What are they saying on the radio?"

"Not much. Mostly military-type transmissions if I can get anything." She looked at him. Obviously she wanted more details – details that would give her answers. "Look, they're not saying much, Molly. And what they are saying ain't good."

Molly frowned. "Jimmy, what do you think happened to Gary? When do you think he'll be home?"

Jimmy put his arm around Molly as he walked her to the edge of his property. "I don't know, honey."

She turned to him before she walked away. "Jimmy, did you put anything else in your little cage?"

He smiled devilishly at her. "Of course I did. I'm not stupid." He turned and walked away without telling her what other saving graces he had in his arsenal.

A sinking feeling settled into Molly's chest as she walked back to her house. *Jimmy's crazy, right? Everything will be up and running any minute now. Heck, it could be on right now!* She couldn't help admitting everything Jimmy said made sense, though, and she didn't like that one bit.

On the third day, there was talk of getting a group together and going to the local grocery store to get what canned and dry goods they could before everything was taken. Molly didn't need anything yet, but she thought it was a good idea. Others might have the same idea, and if they waited too long, there wouldn't be anything left. Jimmy was, of course, better prepared and stayed behind.

She tried not to think too much about the chaos that would ensue if supplies ran out before help arrived. Her mind flashed to Jimmy's shotgun and she shook her head in an attempt to rid herself of the image.

The store was only about two miles away from their street. The city was good about having one every five miles or so, so that no one was too far from what they needed. A few people decided to ride their bikes, equipped with backpacks and baskets, but Molly wanted to walk. She thought it would be too hard to manage heavy supplies and balance on a bike.

When they arrived after about an hour, the doors were locked. One of the men had brought a crowbar, though, and beat the glass until it shattered. Someone else brought a towel that they swept the frame with, making it safe for all of them to pass through. Apparently they were the first to arrive.

After only three days without power, Molly felt odd about breaking into the grocery store this way, but with each passing day, Jimmy became more and more right. With no communication from anyone, who's to say how long it would be? They'd gone longer than that during hurricane season, but they'd had a constant stream of information and knew what to expect. The silence rattled everyone. Even though none of them were desperate, they decided this was the best way to keep the situation from *becoming* desperate. The consensus was that being proactive was the best approach.

So, Molly grabbed some bags from the front of the store and passed out the extras. Then, they fanned out.

The store's front wall was mostly floor-to-ceiling windows, but the other three walls were nothing but cement, so it was pretty dark towards the back. Molly didn't even venture into the freezer section, but she had to go near the meat department to get some pasta. The stench was overwhelming. Rancid pork, chicken, beef and fish filled the air with putrid odors. It threw her gag reflex into overdrive.

She grabbed enough pasta and rice to last awhile and moved on quickly. Guilt overwhelmed her as she filled the cart with dry cereal, dog food, cat food, canned corn, tuna and the like. There was no way to pay for the goods. There wasn't a worker at the place even if they all had cash. Molly decided to tally up everything when she got home and pay for it all when things got back to normal.

She didn't really know how much to take. No one knew how long the power would be out. Some things, like bread, she only grabbed one loaf. Molly knew she wouldn't be able to eat more than that before it went bad. But stuff like cereal that kept longer, she stocked up on. She figured when the power came back in a week or so all of it would still be good, and they'd eat it eventually.

When she got to the pharmacy towards the front of the store, no one else was there. Molly thought about all the neighbors who might need medicines if this went on much longer. She was no doctor though, and didn't know what circumstances might require. She decided to just try to get what she personally might need, and remind everyone to stock up before they left. From in front of the counter she grabbed things like antibiotic ointment, Band Aids, and vitamins – just in case food got scarce, she could still get some nutrition. From behind the counter she grabbed some antibiotics. She stood there thinking about what else she might need, but she couldn't come up with anything. She hoped she wouldn't regret taking so little, as she hopped back over the counter and pushed her overflowing cart to the door.

Several of the neighbors were already there waiting for everyone to finish up, but when Molly mentioned getting medications, they all went back inside.

As she stood alone outside soaking in the sun, she

thought she spotted some movement out of the corner of her eye. It startled her a little, but when she turned to find its source, there was nothing. She glanced around quickly, looking for what she thought she'd seen, and came up empty. It made her a bit uneasy, so she decided to wait inside for everyone. Molly looked back over her shoulder as she turned her cart around, but still didn't see anything.

Her neighbor from the end of the street, Burt, was just walking up as she was coming back in. Burt was a police officer. He hadn't been down to the station since the Blackout, prioritizing his family above work. "Didja forget something?" he asked Molly.

"No, I just wasn't keen on waiting outside alone."

He didn't press Molly for details, but scrutinized the horizon.

It took about an hour, but eventually all were gathered back together at the front of the store, ready to push their carts back home. There was plenty of daylight left to make the trip, so they were in good spirits.

Burt walked next to Molly as they reached the half-way point. "So Burt, not to pry or anything, but how come you didn't go back to the station?"

He was looking straight ahead as he walked and only gave her a sidelong glance and a grunt.

"I mean, it's none of my business, but aren't you worried about work? Couldn't you get in trouble for being a no-show for this long?"

He chuckled, but it was just a noise to make. There was no joy in it. "What makes you think there's anyone there to yell at me?"

"Well, I just assumed, I guess. I mean, isn't your motto 'to protect and serve' or something like that?"

"Yeah well. I guess the job isn't quite as chivalrous as it used to be. And quite frankly, I need to protect and serve my family right now. If the power comes back tomorrow, I'll worry about work then. But that's a big 'if'. Quite frankly, I-" He stopped short when Molly jerked her head to the right.

He looked over that way. "What?"

"I thought I saw something. In fact, I thought I saw it earlier, in the parking lot."

He scanned the area with his dark eyes. The road they were taking was bordered on either side by tree farms. It was nothing but rows and rows of palm trees ready for purchase by wealthy developers.

Someone up front gasped. "I think there's something in the farm," a woman Molly recognized from the next street over said. Molly was trying to think of her name when Burt interrupted.

"What did it look like? Was it an animal?"

It wasn't unheard of to see panthers in the area. But there were enough people that they should've been safe from attack. At any rate, it was unusual for the big cats to attack people. Molly wasn't worried. They were all just a little high-strung from the week's events.

"I'm not sure. It moved away so quickly."

"Where was it?" Molly asked.

She pointed to the farm on the east side of the road. Molly had a bad feeling. *Is there more than one creature stalking us?* She thought.

She looked at Burt uneasily. He frowned. "Just keep moving and stay together."

They were only afforded a few more steps before their assailants made themselves known. Eight men stepped out of the woods from both sides and quickly surrounded the group. They were dressed from head to toe in black, and sweat beaded on their foreheads in the October heat.

"Well now, where do you think you're goin'?" The first one to speak was tan and scruffy looking. His beard was unkempt, and he had a wild look in his eyes. Molly thought by his accent that he might not be from around there. It was more Southern than they were used to. *Maybe they came down from Georgia?* She couldn't tell.

Burt instinctually took command of the situation.

"We don't want any trouble. We're just heading home. Good day to you," he said, and tried to lead the group past the men.

They laughed. "I think all that stuff is too much of a burden for you folks. Let us lighten your load."

Molly glanced around and saw that each of them had something in their hands. One had a long stick that looked like it used to be a broom handle. Another had a crowbar. Another had a baseball bat. All were equally dangerous. All Molly and her neighbors had were groceries. The men shifted their weight menacingly, toying with their would-be weapons.

Burt attempted to reason with them again. "Now, listen. There's plenty of food left at the store. Why don't you guys just go get some for yourselves?"

The one with the mangy beard responded. He seemed to be their leader. "You folks don't want to share? You obviously got all the best stuff, and I was always taught to share if I had something better than my neighbor. I think we ought to teach these folks a lesson."

They closed the circle and Molly started to panic a little. There were more in Molly's group, but they weren't skilled in fighting. Some of the women in the group took the occasional kickboxing class, but that was about it.

They glanced around nervously as the men got closer, and before they could react, Burt made the first move. Apparently he was keeping a pretty impressive knife in his waistband, underneath his shirt. He caught the man closest to him off-guard, and held it to his throat.

"Like I said, we don't want any trouble. If you're looking for food, go get it yourselves."

The man Burt had attacked lifted his chin a little, and Burt responded in kind. A small trickle of blood dripped from the point of Burt's knife.

The leader chuckled, his beard bobbing. "Well, fellas. Looks like we found a group with some spunk." The men laughed nervously, waiting for their leader to tell them what to do.

"Alright. That's fine. We'll go," he said, never breaking eye contact with Burt.

Burt backed off a bit, but kept his knife at the ready. As soon as they opened their circle, Burt led the group through it. The men leered at them as they passed by, but thankfully that was all they did.

It occurred to Molly as they walked away that the men might have had information about other cities, and the conditions in the surrounding areas. She mentioned this to Burt, and he scoffed. "Molly. They were not interested in helping us in any way. In fact, I'm quite certain they would have hurt us, given the opportunity, and if they had been a little hungrier."

"But they might be able to tell us if there's power in other cities. Why we haven't gotten word from anyone yet."

Some of the others in our group perked up when she said that. They were all so desperate for information, it was difficult to let even the smallest chance for knowledge of the outside world slip by.

"What happened here is information enough," he said, a little louder, so others tuning in could hear. He scanned the faces watching them. "Obviously the Blackout isn't an isolated incident. I'd imagine those fellows are wandering around just looking for food. They were probably homeless when the power went out, and didn't have anything stored up like we all did. They have nothing to lose and everything to gain. Their very presence is an indication that our best-case scenario isn't playing out." Burt looked at Molly long enough to make sure she comprehended his point, then he moved ahead.

"Come on, guys. Let's get home to our families."

They picked up the pace and walked the rest of the way home in silence.

How much longer can we survive on speculation of what's going on beyond the city limits? She thought of Jimmy's radio and wondered if he knew the answers. *How much longer will we be kept in the dark?*

9.

The next day, the power was still out. In the morning Gary and Clint raided the airplane's stock and had a fair amount of 'food'. They had ordered cheese and fruit trays for the passengers and ate them first. The chips, nuts, drinks, and candy they hoped wouldn't be needed.

Throughout the day they watched streams of people leave the main terminal buildings, but Clint and Gary stayed put. They walked past the FBO building dutifully, simply following the person in front of them. Gary wondered where they were all going, thinking that not many of them could live within walking distance of the airport.

But then, if my home was only a two or three day's walk from here, I'd have left last night. Maybe. Gary folded his arms over his chest and watched them walking. If the power came back soon, they'd be stuck out there. Gary frowned. *Maybe I'd have stayed put.*

On the third day, Gary concluded no one was coming. He was getting cabin fever, and he was sick of sitting around. The power was still out, and they were living off of vending machine food and the last of the rations from the Hawker. Water was an issue. Luckily there was a river across the field that they could get water from to flush the toilet with, but drinking water would be scarce if the power didn't come back soon. Gary finally broke down after day two and washed off in the river, but it was pretty brisk. It wasn't something he wanted to make a habit of.

He came to the conclusion that they needed to move on from the airport before Clint did. His co-pilot was very duty-oriented and thought they should stay where people knew where they were. Gary just wanted to get back to his family. He wasn't planning on walking the entire way, but he thought maybe they could walk to the closest city that had power.

The airport wasn't that far from I-95, and Gary knew they could walk to Eddystone without too much trouble. He thought they could probably do it in less than a day. Then maybe they could see what was going on and form a plan of attack.

Gary started taking inventory of their supplies and seeing what could be packed and carried. There wasn't an endless supply of food, so one way or another they were going to have to leave soon.

He approached Clint. "Clint, I think we should leave."

"Why?"

"Well, we're running out of food, and haven't seen anyone for days. I think we need to move on from here in order to make some forward progress towards getting home."

"What about the clients?"

Gary laughed. After three days of waiting, Clint was still planning on sitting here. "I don't really give a rat's ass about them, Clint." His volume rose with the frustration of stagnating for the past three days. "I care about not starving to death, and getting back home!" He took a breath. "Besides, even if they aren't just as stranded as we are, and they come waltzing through that door, what are we going to do? It's not like we can take them anywhere."

He let that sink in. "Look, Eddystone is only a few miles from here, and I think it would benefit us to pack up what we have left and start walking."

"Why not go into Philadelphia? It's a bigger city and more likely to offer help, don't you think?"

Gary considered this option, but logically it didn't make sense. "No, I don't think so. If the power has been out at the major metropolitan airport for this many days, the likelihood that it will be on in the city is slim to none."

Clint considered the options, and Gary became impatient. "If you want to stay, I'm not going to stop you. I'll split up the supplies fifty-fifty and you can do what you want. But I sure could use your help. I'm not sure how far I'll have to walk to get information, and it would be nice to have another person along the way." He paused. "At any rate, I'm leaving today. Now, in fact. So, come if you want, or stay. It's your choice."

Gary picked up his backpack and slung the extra bag full of drinks and food over his shoulder. He left two other shoulder bags full of similar supplies on the floor. Clint got up and picked up the bags. "You sure you got everything we need?"

Gary smiled and shook Clint's outstretched hand. "I sure hope so."

They were nervous about walking along 95, so they changed the route a bit. They were both so conditioned to cars driving at high speeds on the highways, neither thought it smart to walk there. So, they decided to take 291 down to Chester, and see what could be found there. If necessary, they could always connect with 95 in Chester.

However, when they started walking along Industrial Highway, it became clear that there were no cars to be afraid of. They were all abandoned and scattered about the road, frozen in that singular moment.

They could tell from the map they'd taken from the lounge that Chester was only about eight miles away. They were both in good shape and set a steady pace. They would easily make it there by nightfall.

It was an eerie walk. No sounds traveled with them. No airplanes, no cars, no horns, no fire truck sirens, no industrial fans, nothing. Just the wind and the occasional sea gull.

Chester was quiet in the twilight air. No one was out and about. Gary looked wearily at Clint as they walked cautiously down the main drag. Every footfall echoed in the evening air as the gravel crunched beneath their feet. All the businesses were abandoned, so if they wanted information it looked like they were going to have to press on, into the rural areas. They checked a few of the restaurants and markets to see if they happened to be unlocked. They could have used some food and additional supplies, but had no such luck.

They didn't have to walk too far to find a neighborhood. A few homes had started to decorate for Halloween. Paper ghosts and skeletons fluttered in the crisp Northeastern air, but with ten days left to Halloween, not too many had carved pumpkins yet, and all were dark, choosing to save candles for inside the house.

The house they chose to approach had a wavering light coming from the windows, indicating they had started lighting candles. Gary hesitated to knock on anyone's door after dark, but they didn't have too many options at this point if they wanted to get out of the elements for the night. Of course, that assumed they would be offered a place to stay.

They approached the door quietly. They could hear people moving around and muffled voices inside. Gary knocked on the door and silence followed. Everyone inside froze. He shifted his weight on the other side of the door and eventually a man with a deep, raspy voice answered the knock.

"What do you want?"

"Mostly information. We're pilots who were stranded

at the airport and we're wondering if you've heard anything about when they're going to start restoring power and operations," Gary answered.

He laughed. "Really. Pilots? That's a new one. Go find someone else to steal supplies from."

"Honestly, sir. We're not trying to steal anything from you. We're both far from our homes and our families, and we'd like to try and find out when we can expect to be reunited with them."

He opened the door a crack, and Gary could see he had wild black hair and a short black beard. His eyes were dark, like the rest of his features. He looked Gary over, taking stock of his uniform and Clint's. "I'm not sure you'll ever see your family again. Now, g'night to you."

He shut the door then, and Gary didn't know what else to do. Then, Clint did something surprising. He knocked on the door. "Please, sir. We could use some help and a dry place to sleep for the night if you're willing. We'll be on our way in the morning."

There was some rustling in the house and the door was eventually opened; however, they were not invited in. A woman now stood next to Black Beard. She was about a head shorter than him, and had blonde hair and a kind look about her.

"Forgive our inhospitality, but there've been some rough folks moving through," she said.

"No apology needed. We understand. Although, we didn't see anyone on our way here. The road was totally deserted," Clint assured her.

She looked at her husband. "Well, that's good news. Maybe most of them have moved on."

The man laughed skeptically. "We'll see about that." He scrutinized us. "How do I know you aren't packing weapons in those packs and intend on shooting my whole family? Hmm? I got my own interests to protect here!"

Gary looked at Clint. "Fine. You're right," Gary said, weighing the options. He decided. "Here." He removed one of the packs from his shoulder and offered it to Black Beard. The door wasn't open wide enough for him to pull it through the door, but the gesture was there. "Search our packs. If you find anything sinister, you keep it to defend your family with."

Black Beard narrowed his eyes. "Wouldn't you keep your protection somewhere that would be easier to get to than buried in a pack?"

They were losing him, and wasting time. Gary turned to Clint and lowered his voice. "Maybe we should just forget it." Clint nodded resolutely.

Before they turned to go, Gary had one last thing to say to Black Beard. "Ya know, I don't know what you folks have been through, but I'd like to think if our situations were reversed I'd offer up some solution, even if it wasn't inviting you into my home. I'm just not the kind of guy who likes to watch people struggle if I can help them in any way."

Black Beard looked over his shoulder and sighed. "Ah, forget it. You might as well come in. We don't have much to offer you, but it might be nice to have some company for a change."

Gary nodded. "Thank you."

They set their packs just inside the door and took a seat in the living room. There were two kids coloring on the floor near the brightest candle. "These are our kids, Barry and Lucy. I'm Karen, and this is my husband Jack."

"Pleased to meet you all. What happened? Why do you say we won't be seeing our families?" Gary asked.

"Oh, now, don't you listen to Jack," Karen replied. "He's a bit of a doomsdayer if you know what I mean. He seems to think this little predicament is more than temporary."

"What makes you say that?"

He puffed on a pipe and sat himself heavily in an armchair nearest the fireplace in the corner. A small fire was happily crackling away. He swept the stem of the pipe from one side of the room to the other. "Look around you. Where is everyone? Where's the cavalry, so to speak? Why has there been no word of recovery? Because everyone is in the exact same boat." He punctuated his statement by pointing the pipe at them with the last three words.

Gary nodded, also fearing that scenario, but hoping he was wrong. "Have you had any information from distant cities? Any other travelers moving through?"

"Nope. Mostly rough folks – thieves and such – probably from the big city. But it seems the situation is the same there."

Gary nodded, his suspicions about Philadelphia confirmed.

Jack got up and went to the other room. He came back with two mugs full of water, some bread, and warm cheese. "We've been trying to finish this cheese up before it goes bad, anyway."

"Well thank you. We've been living off vending machine food for the better part of three days. It'll be good to have something different."

While they chewed, Jack took the opportunity to ask them some questions. "So, what's your plan?"

Gary shrugged. "I'm not really sure. Just keep walking south until we find someplace with power and the ability to get us home."

"And what if you don't find it?"

Clint looked at Gary, wanting the answer just as bad as Jack did. "Then we keep walking. No sense in sitting around. My wife's alone, and if the conditions are the same there, she might get attacked by thieves or God knows what else. I need to get back to her."

"And how far away is your wife?"

"Mine's in Florida. Clint's family is in Georgia."

"Let me get this straight. You're thinking you can walk from Pennsylvania to Florida?" Jack scoffed at the thought.

Gary frowned. He didn't like how quickly this man they'd just met had assessed him. "Like I said, I don't have anything better to do." Gary nodded towards Jack's family and lowered his voice. "I don't have the luxury of having my family right here, and am not afforded the opportunity to dismiss my options so carelessly." He paused, to make sure that sunk in, and brought his voice back to a normal tone. "Anyway, I don't think we'll have to walk that far. Unlike you, I'm optimistic that the situation isn't quite so dire outside of this immediate area."

Jack sighed. "I hope you're right."

"Well, what are you going to do if you're right? Have you got provisions to live this way for the unforeseeable future?" he asked, challenging Jack's mindset.

"No. But we'll have to adapt. I think we can fish the river for food if it comes to that. We can boil water from there too." He put his arm lovingly around Karen. "We'll survive."

Karen smiled. "Anyway, I don't think it's as bad as all that. I don't think the power will just come back on lickety-split, like I thought a few days ago, but I expect to hear some word of help any minute now. I mean, the government must be working towards something. We're not that far from the capital, so surely we'll be among the first to be helped if the problem is more widespread than we might like to think."

"That's true. I hadn't thought of that," Gary said. *Maybe we should stick around,* he thought. He shook his head. *No. We can't wait for someone else to get us home. We have to take a more proactive approach.*

By the look on Clint's face, he seemed to be pondering the same thing, but had come to a different conclusion. He cleared his throat. "Ya know, Gary, maybe she's right. Maybe we should just hang tight here until we get some solid information. Make an informed decision about where to go."

Gary shook his head. "I understand the temptation,

Clint, I really do. But I don't think that's a good idea. Everyone, including the government, has bigger problems than getting us back to our families. I'm afraid if we want to see them again, we're going to have to make it happen for ourselves."

Jack nodded. "You've got that right."

"Well, if you insist on walking, why don't we go to D.C. and see if we can get more information there?"

"What information are you looking for, Clint? It's pretty clear there was some catastrophic failure that caused the power and communication systems to go down. When it comes to our day-to-day survival, does it matter what caused it?"

"No, but it does matter as far as when they're going to get things up and running again. If Karen's right, and they get things going sooner here, we might be able to get a car, or take a train down, or even fly home."

"How long are you willing to wait for that savior?" Gary asked.

Clint didn't answer. It was a difficult choice, and neither of them knew which was the right one. Gary just couldn't bring himself to wait around. He needed to be doing something. He needed to work towards bringing himself closer to his family, even if it was just a mile at a time.

That night, after Jack and his family had gone to bed, Clint and Gary were lying on the couches in the living room.

"I don't want to go any further," Clint said into the darkness.

"That's fine, Clint. It's your life, your decision. I can't make you do anything." Gary dreaded the thought of going on alone, though, and wished Clint would reconsider. At the same time, he didn't need to be wasting energy constantly convincing Clint to stay together. "You know you can't stay with this family, though. They have their own problems, and you can't be a drain on them."

"I know that," he said, obviously offended. "I'll go back to the airport and wait it out there."

"Well, it sounds like you've made your decision. In the morning, we'll go our separate ways." Clint didn't answer, and before too long his breathing evened out and he was asleep. As Gary lay there, he considered everything the family, and Clint, had said. D.C. *was* on the way, and he had it in the back of his mind to stop there, if he made it that far. The power might be on in Baltimore, or somewhere even closer. It would probably take a few weeks to walk there if it came to that, but maybe Clint was right. Maybe he could get more information there. He wondered if he'd have been more open to Clint's suggestion to stop in D.C. if they'd be going on together in the morning. He sighed. Clint hadn't been into this idea from the get-go, and Gary didn't want to waste time convincing him it was a good one. The separation was probably for the best.

Lying on the couch, Gary wished for a lot of things. He wished that he had a weapon of some kind, something more effective than his Leatherman. He wished he had more food and water. He wished he knew if he was going to be able to make this long journey alone. He wished he knew how long it was going to be. Most of all, he wished he was at home with Molly.

Monsters
10.

"Whoever fights monsters should see to it that in the process he does not become a monster. And when you look long into an abyss, the abyss also looks into you."
– Friedrich Nietzsche, *Beyond Good and Evil*

A fight was coming – a fight for human life. Monsters were all around, waiting to pounce on the weak, using the darkness as a veil to hide behind. Those left would have to learn how to fight, and survive. In a world of darkness, a single candle is easily extinguished.

11.

After the encounter with the men on the road, there was a lot of talk about what should be done. It had been about a week since the power went out, and people on the outskirts of town reported more frequent sightings of those deemed "Wanderers" – people looking for handouts, some willing to take them by force.

Burt suggested building a wall around the town. He said in medieval times smaller towns protected themselves against thieves and other outlaws with outer walls, and the same principles could be applied here. Molly thought it was an excellent solution in the long term, but wasn't sure it was what they needed.

After all, the power could come back at any moment, she thought.

Jimmy thought they were all a step behind. He thought they should've already started the wall, he thought they should all be armed and ready to fight for their supplies as things got scarce, and he didn't hesitate to tell Molly. But he refused to speak up to anyone else. He wouldn't leave his house. He was afraid someone would raid his stock if he left. And he wouldn't tell Molly what they were saying on the radio, if anything.

Molly tried to convince him to speak to the people, to help them, but he refused. He said no one would listen when he tried to talk to them before, so why should now be any different? She couldn't help but sympathize with him. But she felt like they'd be so much better off if he would just guide them.

The wall idea, for example. She knew he could help with that, help them plan it out at least. But he wasn't having anything to do with it. Molly didn't see how they were going to do it. And she wasn't entirely convinced it was necessary, not like Jimmy was.

Molly felt another problem with the wall was supplies. Where were they going to get all the materials needed for a huge construction project? Burt suggested raiding the big home improvement stores nearby, and the owner of a local hardware store offered up his stock for the project.

Time was another concern. How long was the wall going to take? The power could be back on before it was finished, and they'll have spent a lot of the local resources trying to build it. Burt argued that if everyone pitched in, they might have it built in under a month.

A month? Molly mused. *Could the power really be off for another month?* Jimmy's warnings echoed in her mind, but she didn't think even he thought it would be out that long.

She brushed her building panic aside and shook her head. "What about know-how, Burt? Who's going to design and actually be in charge of building this wall? I don't know about you, but I'm an English professor. I don't know anything about architecture or how to build a wall that will stand up for any length of time."

"Well, I'm willing to bet that there's someone here who knows about this stuff. Craig, aren't you a general contractor?" Craig nodded, and Burt continued. "You might be able to get us started at least."

Craig looked irritated. "I don't know anything about building a wall from scratch, Burt. You can't just volunteer me for such a giant undertaking and expect me to go along with it. Anyway, why should I waste time on such a ridiculous idea? I have my own family to look out for."

Burt frowned. "Craig, if you help to protect the town, your family will be protected, too."

He scoffed, and all Craig's cronies nodded. "Who died and made you king of the Blackout?" His supporters chuckled.

One of them piped up, "Yeah, we don't have to do anything you say."

Molly could see this wasn't constructive. "Listen. It's only been a week. I say we wait one more week, and if there's still no power and no word from anyone about when this is going to be over, then we start to build. In a few days, we can even start gathering materials if you like. But I just don't want to waste valuable resources if we can help it."

She paused and looked at the hostile dissenters. "Listen, if the power is still out, we'll need to reevaluate. You guys will want to decide which side of the wall you want to be on. Because let me tell you, if you're not willing to help, you're not going to reap the benefits from it, either."

Craig and his companions shifted, exchanging glances at Molly's bold assertion.

With that, it was decided they would wait a week. Molly hoped the power would be back by then, and this wall business would be a non-issue.

It was ten days after the Blackout when it happened – nearly Halloween. It was still warm in Florida, but the nights were nice, and most were comfortable sleeping with the windows open.

They were even starting to adjust to a farming way of life. They went to bed earlier and got up earlier in order to save candles. Most homes were pretty dark inside that night.

Molly was upstairs with Sally and Dug when she heard it. A crash, but it didn't sound close. Dug and Sally weren't bothered by it, but Molly was concerned.

She had been sleeping for at least a few hours. *Who would be moving around at this hour?* she thought.

She went downstairs in her pajamas and peered out the front window, trying to discern the direction the sound came from. That's when she heard the scream, followed by a gunshot.

Molly ran outside towards the noise. Later, she would wonder what she thought she would do in her bare feet, Eeyore pajama pants and a Central Michigan University t-shirt. At the time, though, all she cared about was that someone needed help and she was going to provide it if she could.

However, once she got into the middle of the street, it was quiet again, and she wasn't sure where the sounds had come from. Molly knew they were in front of her, but there were several homes in that general direction. Burt eventually came out of his house a few doors down and saw Molly standing in the street.

"Are you OK? What happened?" he said as he juggled his baseball bat while tying his robe.

"I don't know. It wasn't me. I heard a crash, then a scream and a gunshot, so I came out, but I haven't heard anything since."

They listened to the crickets for a moment longer before a kid ran out between two homes in their direction. "Help! It's my dad!" It was one of the neighbor boys from the next street over. Molly didn't remember what his name was. Their family had a few blonde-headed kids ranging in age from eight to twelve.

They followed him between fences and hedges to arrive at the backyard of his home, where the back door was wide open. There were cries coming from inside. Burt led the way with his baseball bat ready for action.

The boy's mother was sitting on the floor of the

kitchen with her husband's head in her lap. She was crying and stroking his hair. It was dark, but from the flickering candlelight, a dark pool could be seen accumulating under his body. His eyes were closed, but he appeared to be breathing.

Burt dropped the bat immediately and went to the man's side. "What happened here?"

"It was a Wanderer. He broke in, and Kyle came to see what the sound was." She hiccupped a bit, like you do when you're crying hard, and went on. "He had a gun." Hiccup. "Kyle didn't want any trouble," hiccup, "he didn't," hiccup, "even have," hiccup, "anything to," hiccup, "fight him with." She sobbed openly for a few moments.

When she regained some composure, she explained, "By the time I came downstairs the man was running out of the house with an armful of our food."

There was no doctor living in the neighborhood. The best Molly could think of was the woman who worked in the pharmacy. She lived just around the corner.

"Should I go wake Betty?"

Burt looked at Kyle and lifted his shirt. "Probably. Although I'm not sure what she's going to be able to do."

Molly looked at the man, bleeding in his kitchen. "Well, it's the best chance I can think to give him." She turned her gaze to Burt and lowered her voice. "We can't just stand here and watch him die." Burt nodded and she sprang into action.

The boys were hovering around, so Molly gave them something to do. "I need someone to boil some water, and someone else to collect some towels; can you boys do that?" They nodded gravely and set about their tasks.

"I'll be right back," Molly said as she ran out the door.

Molly arrived at Betty's house in record time and banged on the door. "BETTY! WAKE UP! There's been an accident! We need your help! Betty!" It all came out in a single stream, covered over by her rapping on the door.

Betty's husband answered. "Molly. What's this about?"

"George! We need help! Kyle from a few streets over has been shot by a Wanderer. We need Betty to see if there's anything she can do. She was the closest person we could think of."

Betty peered out from behind her husband and nodded. "Just let me get my shoes and a few supplies from the store room."

George sprinted back to the boys' home with them. He didn't like the idea of two women running around in the dark when there was an armed Wanderer on the loose.

By the time Betty arrived, Kyle's breathing was shallow at best. Sandra looked at her with pleading eyes. "Please, you have to help him." The boys had the water boiling and Burt had already applied a few of the towels to the wound in his chest.

"I'll do what I can."

She toiled over him for only a few minutes before he stopped breathing. She instructed Burt to start CPR and explained how to properly administer it while she continued working to stop the bleeding. The candle burned a half-inch of wax while they handed her supplies and tried to help her save Kyle's life. But in the end there was nothing she could do. He might not have survived even with the help of an ambulance. He was shot at close range, right smack in the chest.

Molly had never experienced such tragedy so personally before. The boys cried, their mother cried. Burt, Betty, George and Molly didn't know what to do. They were all grimly considering the implications of what had happened. Why this house? Why this family? Why this night? Where had the Wanderer gone? Was anyone else in the neighborhood in danger?

Burt and George started digging a grave in Sandra's backyard. It may not have been the best burial ground, but the cemetery was several miles away, and the men wanted to busy themselves.

Betty and Molly tried to console Sandra, but what can you say? Just as the sun was coming up, Burt came in to tell Sandra the grave was ready. It was very overwhelming for her. Not twelve hours ago her family was safe in their beds. Molly couldn't comprehend how Sandra's life had been changed so dramatically in such a short period of time. She shuddered to think about how she would have reacted to such a shock, and silently thanked God for the small shred of hope she clung to that Gary hadn't shared Kyle's fate.

A crowd had gathered, and some of the men looked like they'd brought shovels and had been helping dig. Burt, George, and four of Kyle's closest neighbors carried him to the grave. His family followed behind, crying softly. The crowd was mostly quiet, shocked into silence by the night's events.

A few of his friends spoke about what a great father and man Kyle was, and Sandra thanked everyone for coming, but it was inadequate in the end. They were all unprepared in every way for what was taking place.

It wouldn't happen again.

As people were dispersing and Burt was filling in the grave Molly walked over to him. She looked at the remains of Kyle's family, sitting on a bench across the yard. "Build the wall, Burt. Now."

12.

It was Gary's sixth day of walking alone. He fished the river pretty successfully, and hadn't had to tap into his food supply in a while. All things considered, he hadn't wanted for much. He had a supply of lighters to make fires with, the weather hadn't been too terrible so far, and he'd been sleeping under the stars. The biggest problem was drinking water, but that time of year it rained a lot in the North East, so he just had to take time to stop and fill the water bottles when it did.

He was averaging around ten miles per day. If he walked at that pace every day, it would take him just short of three months to get home – if he had to walk the entire way. But he knew walking every day, seven days a week, for ninety days wasn't realistic. He was bound to have to stop for one reason or another. He'd get sick, a bad storm might come, some distraction was liable to present itself. He still hoped he wouldn't have to walk the entire way, though. Eventually he had to get far enough away from the epicenter, right? Assuming, of course, that Philadelphia had been the epicenter.

It'd been about ten days since the power went out, and so far, each town he'd come to was the same. No power, no friendly faces. In fact, there weren't too many people moving around at all. Gary heard whispers of people who were being called nomads, wanderers, and other less pleasant things. They were thieves and people who might take your supplies from you, and people who didn't have a home to protect. It occurred to him that he was a Wanderer, and he wondered how that stigma might impact his journey.

When Clint and Gary had parted ways in Chester, he followed 495 south, so he could stay nearer to the coast. Then he caught back up with I-95 south of Wilmington, in Delaware. He loved that about the Northeast. The states were so small, he really felt like he was making good progress, even if it was only about ten miles per day.

Gary decided that even though 95 took him away from the coast for a few days, he needed to stick with it, based on the fact that he didn't want to walk the perimeter of Delaware just to get a fresh meal every day. He caught up with Chesapeake Bay in no time, though, and spent the night on the north side of the bridge.

By his calculations, he only had about thirty more miles before he reached the outskirts of Baltimore. He was counting heavily on finding more information there. It was the biggest city he'd come to so far, and someone there had to have information about what was going on, if the power was out there. It might even be on, that many miles away from Philly. His mind was reeling at the prospect and he had trouble sleeping that night.

It took Gary three and a half days to close the distance between the Bay Bridge and Baltimore. Because he wasn't following the coast as much anymore, his supplies were running low, and he was hoping to restock in the big city.

It was nearly two weeks since the Blackout. People seemed to be becoming more and more hostile as time went on, or as he traveled further south, he wasn't sure which. Although there were more people milling around in the city proper, no one made direct eye contact. In fact, most folded their arms protectively over their chests, and watched Gary out of the corners of their eyes. No one seemed approachable. Some even looked like they might lash out if they were challenged.

He sighed heavily. This wasn't the situation he'd imagined. Obviously the power was out there, as it was everywhere else.

And there was a new problem brewing. After so many miles of walking in his work shoes, not only were his feet becoming tired and blistered, the soles of his shoes were wearing thin. He had a roll of duct tape that he patched them with, but he knew that wouldn't last. He had to come up with a new pair of shoes soon. He was discouraged that his shoes were already wearing out. He wasn't even out of the Northeast yet.

At this rate I'll need over ten pairs of shoes to make the journey. He shuddered at the thought, and reminded himself that he was still hopeful that he wouldn't have to walk the entire way. *Perhaps the next city will be different. Perhaps.*

Gary spent the night in an alley on the outskirts of Baltimore, and it was anything but restful. It was cold in Baltimore that time of year, and he did his best to conserve body heat. He curled up in a spot he thought would be out of the way, but he was wrong- the alley he picked belonged to someone. Lucky for him, he'd taken to sleeping with his packs under his coat, so they couldn't be stolen while he slept. Just as he was drifting off he was grabbed by the collar and jerked to his feet by a rather large man. Gary was no slouch at over six feet tall, but this guy had bulk.

"Whaddya think you're doin?" The bulky fellow asked. Gary was so groggy it took a moment to process what he was asking through the thick accent.

He socked Gary in the gut. "I asked you a question."

The breath quickly fled Gary's lungs and he doubled over. He put his hand up to try and stem further assaults and the man backed up a step. "Well?" he asked.

"I'm just … passing through." Gary gasped. "I didn't mean to cause trouble."

"This alley's taken. See that you keep passing, huh?"

"Sure. No problem." Gary started to limp away, but he turned. It was the first conversation he'd had with anyone in a few days, and despite the obvious hostility, he thought it was worth a shot to ask him if for information.

"You stupid or somethin'? Move along!" In the dark, it was difficult to make out any features besides the outline of his bulky body. His voice was loud, deep and had a bit of a gravel to it. It was intimidating enough that Gary nearly turned back around, but he couldn't lose this chance.

"Have you guys heard anything?"

"Bout what?"

"About what's going on. About when things will start going back to normal, about when we might hear some news, about when we might get some relief." Gary looked at his shadow as the big man laughed.

"There is no relief. This is the situation, so you better learn to survive. You can start by moving along."

"How do you know that?"

"Look around you! It's anarchy! No one's coming to help you." He approached Gary menacingly.

Gary took a step back and cleared his throat. "Thanks." He hated to turn his back, but he thought it might placate the man, so Gary turned and started walking.

This wouldn't do. He had to find some place to rest or his progress tomorrow would be even slower.

Eventually he came across an empty shop. It had already been broken into, and there was glass everywhere by the sound his footsteps were making. He walked around the little shop as quietly as he could. He didn't want to surprise anyone if there was someone already sleeping here. He wished he had a flashlight that worked. By the lack of response to Gary's presence, he could only assume there wasn't anyone else in the shop. So, he found a spot in the back corner of the store and laid down. That gave him as much time as possible to hear someone approaching. It was a restless night, though, despite the fact that he didn't see anyone else. He was rattled by the encounter with the bulky man in the alley. It seemed like the situation- his situation, the U.S.'s situation, humanity's situation, - was becoming more dire by the day.

It occurred to Gary rather suddenly, as he lay there in the dark listening, that for the first time in his life, he'd completely missed a holiday. He'd forgotten all about Halloween, and had done nothing to observe it. Although he and Molly didn't have kids, they always passed out candy – assuming of course that he was home. If he was on the road, he listened to Molly tell him which neighbor kids had dressed up as what that night. Last year's popular costumes were princesses, werewolves, and the latest animated movie character. Gary couldn't remember what the thing's name was.

Normalcy. I missed out on something normal, he thought.

You could argue he hadn't had anything normal in over two weeks. No showers, no regular meals, no transportation, no phone calls. But a missed holiday?

Gary sighed and rolled over, trying not to focus on the situation as a whole, but on his immediate condition, and the fact that he needed sleep.

In the morning, he took out the map to study it more closely. He still had about a half-day's walk until he was the other side of Baltimore. He had two choices, as he saw it. He could either keep on his original course and follow I-95 all the way home, or he could take the more rural roads along the coast. That way, he'd at least have more consistent access to food. But winding along the coast would also take longer, and would keep him away from most of the bigger cities. He hadn't decided if that was good or bad yet. After the experience in Baltimore, he wondered if he should avoid the big cities for now.

But how will I ever find some place that has power if I do that? he thought.

It was less than forty miles to D.C. The capital had to have something- information, supplies, anything. It was the government's responsibility to care for the people. They had to have some station set up with supplies, people to talk to, military officials offering assistance, things like that. So Gary folded the map and started on his way, decision made. In four days, he expected answers.

13.

Construction on the wall began immediately, but not without dissent. Craig and his group of naysayers were entirely opposed to building the wall, even after the attack. They argued it would take too long, would be more work than it was worth, and didn't want to contribute their time and supplies to something that would be useless by the time it was finished, since they expected the power to be restored by then.

Burt heard their arguments calmly and gave them two options. They could either suck it up and help out, or move their families outside the areas zoned for the wall and save their supplies and energies for their own families. Craig was the loudest voice against the wall.

"What right do you have to order me to abandon my home?" he yelled.

"If you aren't going to contribute to this community, you can leave," was Burt's response.

"Who died and made you my boss, hmm? You don't own my home, I do! You have no business kicking me out!" He shook with rage.

Burt remained calm and reasonable. "I do if you're going to be a leech on this community and its very limited supplies. You're more than welcome to stay if you want to contribute."

Craig lowered his tone and narrowed his eyes at Burt. "You think you're so smart, do ya? Well, what are you going to do when this 'community' collapses on itself, and it's every man for himself? What then, huh, fearless leader?"

Burt ignored the threat entirely. "What is your decision? We're starting work on the wall in the morning. Either show up to help, or be gone by then."

"And what are you going to do if I squat in my house?"

He had a point. Molly wasn't sure what Burt could do if he decided to just hang around inside his house, steal supplies and otherwise cause problems.

"I'll be forced to relocate you myself. Please don't let it come to that. I have better things to do." Burt turned and walked away, leaving Craig in the middle of a crowd that passed judgment on him with every gaze.

He looked spastically from person to person. "Mark my words, this'll be the death of you all." The crowd parted for him so he could storm off.

At the edge of the group, Molly noticed Jimmy watching the scene with a frown on his face. He turned to walk back to his home, and Molly yelled for him.

"Hey! Jimmy!" He kept right on walking. "Jimmy! Wait up!" She caught up to him just a short distance from his house. "Hey," she said, breathless.

He nodded in response.

"Whaddya think?"

"Not much."

"Really, Jimmy? Come on! Throw me a bone here! I know you have some kind of opinion on what's happening with the wall, and Craig, and everything!"

"Yup. Not sure if I wanna share it with you, though."

Molly looked over to find a mischievous glint in his eye. She smacked him on the arm. "Well, you better get your mind right, 'cuz I wanna know. It's dark enough around here without you trying to pull the covers over my eyes!"

He laughed. "I think Craig is gonna be a problem, no matter what he decides."

Molly had the same feeling. "What about the wall? Don't you think the power will be on by the time we're done with it?"

"No, I don't. And what does it matter if it is? Gives folks a chance to feel like they're doing something to help, to protect themselves. Why take that away?"

Molly hadn't thought of that. "I suppose if it is back on in the next few weeks, we can always disassemble it and reuse the supplies as we need them."

"Yup."

They stopped at the end of Jimmy's driveway. "It just seems like such a permanent solution."

Jimmy turned toward Molly and put his hand on her shoulder. "Honey, we're looking at a permanent problem. The world is changed, and whether for the worse or better remains to be seen."

Molly harrumphed at that. "Isn't there any good news coming from that radio of yours?"

He frowned, remaining tight-lipped.

She sighed. "Jimmy, why save that thing if you're not going to tell anyone you have it, and what they're saying?"

He looked her in the eye. "To be ready."

She wasn't sure what he meant by that. She shifted her weight from leg to leg. "Well, at any rate, see ya tomorrow at the wall!"

Jimmy turned and waved as he headed up his driveway.

In the morning, they all gathered to begin the wall's construction. Craig had decided to leave, and had done so quietly, but Molly feared it wasn't the last they'd see of him.

They were lucky that the neighborhood was fairly small, and they calculated they would need to create a square that was about a mile long on each side, four miles of wall total. They estimated a week for each side of the wall, totaling a month of construction.

They sent messengers to the outlying, more rural homes to let them know that they would be on the outside of the wall, and they were more than welcome to move in and settle on the inside. Most said no. They were used to being on their own, and weren't interested in moving in with strangers. Molly couldn't blame them, but she was afraid it was a choice they would regret before too long.

At first, everyone in town was designated to gather supplies. They did that for two days straight. They gathered rocks from the beach and cut trees from the nearby tree farms. Although most of those were palm trees, they still worked for good solid planks of wood once they were cut down. Molly carried rocks mostly. She would collect as many big rocks as she could in the wheelbarrow she was given and bring them back. Round trip, it took about forty-five minutes, but she could gather a fair amount at once. Over the course of those two days she made about twenty round trips to the beach. During the trips, she couldn't help but wonder about Cindy and what she was doing at that moment. Was she safe? How was her family? Was her community doing the same thing they were? Molly hoped so. Cindy lived too far away to go visit, so all Molly could do was hope her dear friend was all right.

By the end of two days gathering supplies Molly was exhausted, but there was no time to quit. Construction began immediately.

It had been sixteen days since the Blackout, and even though no Wanderers had been seen since the night Kyle was murdered, they were wary. There was a constant sense of unease, and they were all in a hurry to get the wall finished for that added security.

The town celebrated Halloween the night before the official construction started. Some of them just happened to have candy on hand, and some didn't have anything to spare, but just wanted to see the children in their costumes. They agreed no one should be out wandering after dark, so the kids started knocking around four and quit by six-thirty. Molly felt it was nice to have a small taste of something normal. It served as a reminder that life does go on, that traditions remain despite disaster and tragedy.

But, much like any holiday, it was back to work the next day. They labored for the next two weeks on the wall. They mixed mortar from the nearby hardware store, they dug the foundation, and they assembled it under the direction of some of the contractors who lived in the neighborhood.

Then, it happened.

It was the middle of the night when a group of four Wanderers came into the neighborhood. They had stationed people around the area to guard the supplies just in case, and the alarm they raised cut through the night like thunder.

Molly was on her feet at once with the gun Burt had given her. Dug jumped up, growling, and Sally ran to hide under the bed. It was the first time Dug had demonstrated such aggressive behavior, and Molly wasn't sure how to react. She ran for the door and Dug followed.

"No Dug, you need to stay here. I don't want you to get hurt," she told him and gave him the signal for 'stay'. He wasn't having it, though, and stayed right on her heels. There wasn't much time to react, so she ended up letting him follow.

Once she entered the darkness, she had a hard time perceiving what was going on. It seemed like the commotion was a few streets over. There wasn't any immediate danger to Molly or Dug. She was tempted to go back inside and wait it out, but she knew that if she were the one in trouble she wouldn't want everyone to hide out and let her deal with it herself. So, she padded as quietly as possible toward the commotion.

By the time Dug and Molly arrived, everything seemed to be under control. She saw Burt and ran to him. "What happened?" Dug changed his attitude immediately upon seeing Burt and became friendly and joyous once again.

Burt patted Dug on the head distractedly. "We were attacked. Three Wanderers came and tried to take some of our supplies. Seemed like when they realized it wasn't food they moved on. Betty said she thought she saw four at first, but there's been no sign of a straggler."

"Did they get any of our food?" Molly asked wearily. Most families were still keeping their food in their own homes, which would lead the Wanderers to their front doors.

"I don't know yet. I hope not." He spoke into the darkness, never really making eye contact with Molly, but constantly scanning for additional dangers.

"Well, what can I do?"

"The best thing? Probably go back to your home and make sure it's secure. I can send someone with you if you'd like."

"No, I'll be OK. The original attack was so far from our street, I think we'll be fine."

Molly walked back home feeling relieved, and hoping the incident remained minor.

But as she approached the front walk she could tell something wasn't right. Dug bristled and the hair on his neck stood on end. He growled loudly and she readied her gun, a small hunting rifle Burt had taught her to use.

The door was open slightly, and she pushed it the rest of the way with the barrel of the gun. It was dark inside, and Molly couldn't tell what was a shadow and what was actual movement. At first, she pointed the gun wildly from corner to corner of the room. Then she took a deep breath and slowly moved farther into the house.

Everything was silent, save for Dug's low growl. He pointed his nose to the air, whimpered and took off towards the bedroom. "Dug!" Molly hissed, but he didn't listen, so she took off after him.

She rounded the corner to the bedroom and the smell of blood hit her like a ton of bricks. The only light she had was the moonlight shining through the window, so she carefully walked to the window and opened the curtains to try and shed more light on the room.

In the center of the floor by the bed Molly saw Dug bathed in pale light. He was standing over a grisly scene. A pool of blood and clumps of fur were all that remained. Molly sucked in a breath. "Sally…" she breathed.

Molly grabbed the gun and darted back out the way she came. Out in the street she scanned both ways for movement. Any sign of her beloved, and probably horribly injured, pet. But she had disappeared. Molly could hear Dug howling from inside the house. She fell to her knees in the street and cried. She had left her there alone.

It's my fault she died so horribly, Molly thought. *They probably wanted her for the meat, but I'd rather they starved.*

Jimmy was making his way back to his own home after helping defend the supplies when he stumbled upon Molly in the middle of the street. He ran to her. "Molly, what's happened?" He held his gun up defensively and scanned the horizon.

"Sal-ly," she hiccupped. "They-killed-her."

"Oh." He didn't have any pets of his own and didn't know how to relate to this outpouring of emotion over a cat, so he cut to what he thought was more important. "What about your food? Did they get any of it?"

She thought, hiccupping every few moments. *I didn't check my food. I was so worried about Sally I didn't look to see if they'd gotten any of my food.* A new level of panic rose, and she sprang to her feet and ran to the house. Dug was still howling upstairs and Jimmy frowned at the sound. Molly went to the garage, where she was keeping her food. She figured it was an unconventional place and hoped it would discourage thieves, because they would have to search for it.

She'd put locks on the cabinets, hoping that would deter thieves even further. Locks take time to break. Lucky for Molly, the locks were undisturbed. She sighed heavily and Jimmy put his hand on her shoulder. "Well, there's a blessing."

"Yes, well. I had to sacrifice my cat to get it." She turned to look at him. His eyes were big, green and full of uncertainty. He was single, and not used to dealing with emotionally unstable women. "They killed her in my bedroom! That's were Dug is."

He put his arm around her and led her out of the garage. "I'll stay here tonight if it'll make you feel better. I can sleep on the couch, OK? In the morning, I'll help ya clean up."

"I can't sleep in there tonight, Jimmy!"

"Don't ya have a guest room you can use?"

"I s'pose," she pouted.

"Look, it'll be OK. You've still got all of your food, and hey, you've got Dug." Dug howled upstairs. "It could've been worse. What if you'd been here? What do you think they would've done to you?"

"I sure would've made it harder for them to hurt Sally."

He shook his head, seeing this was a losing battle. "Why don't you go get in bed? Hashing it out isn't going to change anything."

That night, she sobbed into her pillow as Dug lay by her side. Though her sobs, she asked Dug, "Where is your father? Why isn't he here? He would never have let this happen."

Dug only whimpered a reply as she soaked the pillow with tears.

14.

It was a long four days to D.C. The trek took him far from the coast, and Gary had run out of food by the time he reached the city. It was a wet few days though, so at least he wasn't wanting for water.

The situation in D.C. seemed similar to Baltimore at first. But soon Gary saw it was different. Horribly different. As in Baltimore, the power was clearly off, and the place had been looted right down to the building studs, but there was no one. It was an absolute ghost town.

Garbage and debris littered the streets and sidewalks that wove their way through the capital city. Gary's lone footsteps echoed off buildings and disappeared into nothingness. No aid for the country's citizens. No information for those left. Nothing.

He kicked a small rock a few feet and listened to it bounce along the street. When he caught up with it, he picked it up and examined it.

What is going on? Why is this happening? What did I do to deserve such abandonment? He flung the rock at the nearest window. It was already broken and went sailing through, landing in what remained of the storefront. It wasn't very satisfying, to tell the truth.

Deflated, he decided to fish the river near the Washington Mall for a bit. He tripped and fell spectacularly on the way to the riverbank. He clenched his teeth and stood up, brushing the front of his pants off, not having much luck with the mud and grass stains that found a new home on his clothes.

While Gary was readying the fishing line, he cut his hand open with the hook.

That's it. I've had enough. He stood up, picked up the pack and flung it as far as it would go. What was left of his supplies spilled out as the pack arched over the field. He fell to his knees and cried while he watched it fall. But there was no one to see him cry. No one to comfort him. No one to answer his questions. Gary lost track of time while he knelt there, tears streaming into his newly-grown beard. He finally allowed himself to mourn the losses of the last few weeks.

When the tears stopped, he took a deep breath and stood. He gathered everything that had spilled out of the pack and collected the bag from the other side of the field. Then he renewed his effort to catch some fish, and made a fire in a grassy field overlooking the Washington Monument. He feasted on fresh fish – his first real meal in about thirty-two hours. As twilight settled in, exhaustion overwhelmed him. He found a secluded spot near the Lincoln Memorial, and was asleep before he could even lay his head down.

Gary felt something poking him. He opened one eye, and couldn't see anything. A light was shining in his face, with nothing but darkness beyond it. He brought his hands to his face to shield his eyes. "What the hell?"

"Don't move." A nondescript male voice commanded.

He froze. *Shit. What now?*

"What are you doing here?"

"Trying to get some sleep. I was having pretty good

luck until you fellas came along."

"Sir, the only thing his pack has that could be considered a weapon is a multi-purpose knife. Everything else appears to be simple supplies." That voice seemed younger than the first, but it was hard for Gary's startled mind to know for sure. The light made it impossible to see.

"Not a threat?"

"No, sir. Not immediately."

"Copy that."

His pack landed roughly in his lap. "Move along now. We've got orders to shoot on sight anyone who doesn't belong here. Consider this your one and only warning."

"But," Gary paused. "What? I mean, where can I go? Is everywhere like this? How will I know where's safe?"

The men didn't answer. He watched the light become dimmer as they backed away. He never saw them clearly, just shadows and silhouettes. He thought he caught the outline of a gun on more than one of them, and helmets on them all.

The military, he thought. *It's worse than I thought.*

When he felt like they were far enough away, he threw his pack over his shoulder and started trying to navigate the darkness. He still felt like they were watching him, but he didn't see any sign of them by the light of the moon.

He walked to what he hoped was a little beyond the borders of D.C. and set up his camp for the second time that night.

In the morning he knew he had to come up with a plan. He pulled out the map and considered his options: stick with I-95 all the way home, or follow the coast. After what he'd seen in D.C., and how hard it was to come by food away from the coast, he was leery of straying from it again. He looked more closely at his map and saw that a rural road skirted the shoreline pretty closely most of the way. Gary decided loosely following that was his best bet.

He hoped staying away from the bigger cities would keep him under the military's radar.

He decided not to think too much about his long-term problems: supplies, the state of his shoes, how long he'd last on his own. To survive, he had to be concerned with now. Today. What was he going to do to get as far south as he could in that one day? That became his new mantra.

He had learned to take it one day at a time during a special workshop on survival. He thought it was important to learn what to do if his plane ever did go down in the middle of nowhere, and he survived. It had been the longest five days of his life – up until the Blackout, at least. He and four others were dumped in the middle of the swamp with one instructor, who taught them how to hunt, how to start a fire, how to build a shelter, and how to stay alive. Gary was left bit to hell by mosquitoes, cut to hell by the thick brush they had to trudge through, and tired as hell after sleeping in hammocks made from palm fronds so they could get up off the ground at night. The first night, he hadn't quite perfected his hammock construction yet, and he came crashing down into the swamp below around two a.m. Sputtering and scrambling to get out of the alligator-infested waters, he didn't sleep much the rest of that night. But it was all worth it. Knowledge he hoped he'd never have to use was coming in very handy during this long journey.

He made it into Virginia easily and stopped for the night inside a wildlife preserve. He thought back to some show he'd watched on the Discovery Channel before all this happened. That guy had made trapping animals look so easy. Gary tried his hand at a few snares before he went to bed, but came up empty in the morning.

He frowned at the empty trap. *Not as easy as I'd hoped.*

He ended up fishing the river again, and although he wasn't hungry after the meal, he had been hoping to have something other than fish for breakfast.

As he cast the bones and skin into the fire he said aloud, "I s'pose I should be grateful for the meal." Gary sighed. He *was* grateful. It had been eighteen days since the Blackout. He was a Wanderer, but he was alive. He could only hope Molly's conditions were a little better.

15.

Three weeks into the wall's construction, a fire broke out. The alarm rousted everyone from their beds in the middle of the night. Molly caught up with Jimmy, standing on the edge of the blaze.

It looked like a bonfire, near where they were constructing the third section of the wall. Molly was confused.

"What's going on?"

"Someone set fire to the supplies," Jimmy said, so flatly that it caught Molly off-guard.

"What? Oh my God! We have to put it out! Maybe some of the ones in the middle of the pile are still usable!" She looked around. "Where's Burt?"

Jimmy gestured. "Over there."

Molly abandoned Jimmy's nonchalance and ran to Burt. "Burt! What can I do? How can we get this out?"

Burt looked mournfully at the blaze. "I don't think we can. Best thing is to just let it burn out. The supplies are a loss."

"No! Come on! Maybe there's some salvageable things in the middle that haven't been burned yet! I'll go get some buckets and we can put it out!" She looked at

Burt, and lowered her voice. "Burt, please. Don't give up like this."

He turned and simply looked at her.

"Who did this?" she demanded.

"We think it was a group of Wanderers."

Molly shook her head. "That doesn't make any sense. Wouldn't Wanderers take the supplies, rather than destroy them?"

Burt grunted a response.

"Burt-"

But he cut her off. "Molly, you know as much as I do. Now, I have things to do. I'll see you in the morning."

She was left standing alone in the moonlight. Jimmy approached quietly. "I don't understand," she said.

"Honey, I'm not sure any of us do."

The next day, they scrambled to try and replace the lost supplies. While they scrounged, rumors flew about who was responsible. It turned neighbor against neighbor, as everyone suspected it was someone inside who'd done it. Otherwise, why not take the supplies, as Molly had suggested?

Molly didn't fully agree. Her theory was that Craig was behind the whole thing. She thought he'd gotten some of his cronies to help him sneak back into the town and start the fire.

She was taking a break near the town square when a fight broke out. "Well, I'll bet you started it!" someone yelled at another person standing nearby.

"Why the hell would I do that? Because I love manual labor so much I wanted to extend our work?" The accused man was big and tan, an imposing sight to Molly.

The accuser had sharp features, a pointed nose, and chin. Even his hair met in a point at the back of his neck. He just looked weasely to Molly, like a used-car salesmen. The closer she looked at him, the more he seemed like one of Craig's cronies, but she couldn't be sure. "You tell me!"

he shouted.

The big man began to close the distance between them. "You get this straight. I've been here every day helping to build this wall to keep my family and horse-shit like you safe." By then he was on top of the weasel and jabbed his oversized finger into the smaller man's scrawny chest. "Make no mistake. I didn't have anything to do with that fire."

The tension was immense. Molly spotted Jimmy in the distance. He was supposed to be cutting trees into more manageable pieces, but he'd stopped to observe the fight. His ax dangled by his side as he scrutinized the scene.

The men stared at each other, and Molly wasn't sure what to do. The weasel wasn't someone she would trust if a fight did break out. The accused had bulk though, and wasn't someone she'd want to be in the way of, either.

While she tried to decide if she should step in, the fight diffused itself. The weasel simply backed away from the big man. He made no apology, but he didn't make any more threats either. The big man just watched him walk away.

She let out a breath she didn't realize she'd been holding and tried to get back to work. It was hard, though, with people's anger simmering just below the surface.

Quiet
16.

"It is so quiet and peaceful, and I sit here, and ponder, and am restless. It is the quiet that makes me restless. It seems unreal. All the world is quiet, but it is the quiet before the storm. I strain my ears, and all my senses, for some betrayal of that impending storm. Oh, that it may not be premature! That it may not be premature!"
– Jack London, *Iron Heel*

The quiet that enveloped the world was suffocating. There was no whisper of what happened. No hum of machinery. No song of hope. And in that quiet, all a body can do is think.

17.

It took about a week to recoup the supplies. They had to go farther out of town to get trees, which took longer to bring back, and made them all nervous.

Once their pile was restored, Burt called a town meeting.

"Now look, everyone," he started. "We need a serious attitude adjustment." Murmuring spread through the crowd. "We do! What happened was a minor setback, but if we let it, it will poison us. We can't turn on each other over it! No one was hurt, and that's what's important. There's no way to prove or disprove what happened, although I've heard a lot of theories floating around, and far too many accusations." He looked hard at someone in the crowd. Molly followed his gaze to the weasel. "We've been able to recover nicely from the incident, and I don't want to hear any more about it, is that clear?"

The weasel spoke up. "I don't have to stand here and be chastised like a child. Who appointed you the leader of this band of misfits? Maybe Craig had the right idea!"

Burt bristled. "If you want to follow in Craig's footsteps, be my guest."

A voice spoke up. "Burt, he may have a point. Might

be we should take a vote for who should serve as our leader." Molly's mouth hung open at Jimmy's words, shocked that he was finally getting involved.

"And I suppose you would like the job, Jimmy?"

"Hell no, I don't. I think you're doing the best you can with what you've been given. But, if you were fairly elected by the majority, it would certainly shut these idiots up." He gestured towards the weasel when he said it.

Burt considered. "Jimmy, you may have a point. Tomorrow, we'll vote on who should lead this town, since there have been so many complaints. Each person is to bring a piece of paper with a name on it. Whoever has the most votes in the end wins, and can take over. Sound good to everyone?"

Heads bobbed in nervous ascension. Molly frowned. *What if the weasel gets elected? We'll self-destruct before the power has a chance to come back.*

Molly spent a restless night trying to decide what she would do if the weasel did get elected. If she left, how would Gary find her? If she stayed, would she survive the coming weeks? She'd wanted to talk to Jimmy about it, but he'd left before she could catch up to him. *What would he do?* she wondered.

The next day, she walked to the square with her scrap of paper in hand. They'd decided to tally the votes there. She felt Jimmy would do a better job than Burt, but knew he didn't want the job. So, she'd scribbled Burt's name on the scrap before she left the house, and jammed it into the jar filled with other slips of paper. Voting would conclude at sunset. Then the votes would be counted, and a winner announced. In the meantime, everyone was to stick to their tasks, unless they were going to vote.

That evening, everyone gathered at the square. Molly had been chosen to help count the votes, and she read the results to the crowd.

"Burt won by a landslide. He took over eighty percent

of the votes."

A cheer rose up. When it died down, the weasel had something to say. "Who came in second?"

"Does it really matter? It wasn't even close," Molly responded.

"It matters to me!" He shouted.

"Fine. Jimmy Jean took ten percent, and the rest were just single votes, or people who just had a few. Happy?"

Jimmy looked surprised, and the weasel was enraged. She guessed that was her answer.

"Look, Burt is a former police officer. He's the most qualified for the job." Molly paused. "Certainly more qualified than you," she said under her breath.

The weasel took a step forward, but the crowd closed around him, barring his way.

Burt quickly moved beside Molly at the front of the crowd and cleared his throat. "OK. Now that that is done, tomorrow we get back to work. I want this wall done, and I want it done yesterday."

Most everyone cheered, except the weasel.

In the end, it was about five weeks before the wall was totally finished. The fire only set them back a week, and they were left with a wall that made them proud. It was something Molly knew would keep them safe. But for how long? She couldn't believe the power was still out when they finished.

It had been fifty-one days since the Blackout. Fifty-one days of silence. Fifty-one days without hearing from Gary. Fifty-one days of not knowing.

Once the wall was finished, they allowed themselves a small celebration. It was only a few days until Thanksgiving, so the festivities were set for the same time. They roasted a wild boar someone had shot outside the wall, someone played music on their guitar, and they sang. It boosted morale remarkably.

At the same time, though, it was depressing for Molly.

It wasn't her first Thanksgiving without Gary by any stretch of the imagination. They'd been married nearly ten years, and for all of them he'd been a pilot. Quite frankly, she was lucky to get any holidays with him. But it was her first Thanksgiving totally alone, and her first without any communication at all from him. If he was going to be gone for a holiday, he usually did something special, to remind Molly that even though he loved his job and it was important to him, he really wanted to be with her on that special day. One year he sent a bouquet of daisies with a nice note. Another year he left a copy of *Pride and Prejudice* for her to watch – Molly's favorite movie – and a Post-It that said, *Wish I was here to watch it with you, Mrs. Darcy.* Over the years, she'd come to depend on his love.

But this year, she'd get nothing. No call, no flowers, not even a text message. And despite the fact that Molly knew that going into the day, she still felt like crying when she went to bed that night.

Burt decided the next big project post-wall-building should be a town well. He wanted to build it in the center of town, so everyone had access to it, and could get fresh water without having to boil it. The well didn't take very long though, and was finished in under a week.

In the days that followed they were all given tasks. Some guarded the wall. Others farmed a small plot inside the wall, and a larger one on the outside. They debated the placement of these farms, as Wanderers could take food as they wanted. In the end though, there wasn't enough space inside the wall for everyone to be well-fed, and they figured sacrificing some food to the Wanderers was better than being malnourished for the duration.

Jimmy was appointed to the post of Watcher, to defend the wall, and Molly worked the farm on the inside of the wall. Because of its size, there were only two that tended it. The weather was cooling off with the start of December, so Molly didn't really mind working outside every day. They plowed, planted, weeded, carried water from the well daily to make sure the crops didn't get too dried out, and tried to keep bunnies and other small pests away from it. She even asked Jimmy to show her how to set up traps, so she could catch them if any came too close. As more time passed, it seemed a waste to just scare them away. Meat was scarce, and rabbit was good eating, if you could get past how cute they were.

Tending the farm wasn't really an all-day job, but it kept them busy. And since everything else seemed to take longer without the comforts of electricity, Molly was fine with less than a full day of work. By the time she got home, stoked a fire, cooked a hot meal, washed clothes, cleaned the house, and anything else that needed to be done, it was dark and time for bed.

It was a mundane life, but at least it was safe. No one had been hurt by a Wanderer since the wall's completion. There had been plenty of attacks, and the farm outside of the wall had been looted a number of times, but everyone was safe.

It was around day sixty-two when Burt approached Molly about a school.

"Listen, Molly. Some of the parents have been talking. We're getting well into December here, and haven't had any news of when things will be getting back to normal. So we were thinking maybe we should start teaching the kids on our own."

"What do you mean?"

He shifted his weight, nervous about approaching her on the subject. "Well, like having a school, ya know? So the kids don't get too far behind?"

"Burt, first of all, that's a fairly permanent solution to a fluid problem. The power could come back on tomorrow."

He raised his right eyebrow, but Molly persisted. "Second, you've got such a wide variety of ages in town. How could you accommodate them all?"

"We just thought that something would be better than nothing."

Molly sighed, really thinking about this idea. It was ridiculous. If they did this, it was like admitting the power was never coming back, that they were truly on their own.

"Hey, if the power comes back -"

Molly interrupted him. "When the power comes back."

He cleared his throat. "Right. When the power comes back, the kids can go back to school. No harm done. It'll just give them something to do during the day besides chasing rabbits, and building rope swings, which, by the way, I think every yard in the neighborhood is equipped with at this point."

Molly smiled. Last week they'd hung one in her yard, and she didn't even have kids.

"Where do you intend to hold the school? It'd have to be someplace large enough to house them all."

"Well, when it comes down to it, there really aren't that many school-aged kids inside the wall. Forty, maybe fifty tops. So I was hoping maybe we could do it at someone's house."

Now it was Molly's turn to raise an eyebrow. "Whose house did you have in mind?"

He cleared his throat again. Molly would've thought he was coming down with something if he wasn't so nervous-looking. "Yours, maybe?"

"What? Whoa, Burt, hold your horses here. I'm a college English professor. I don't know anything about teaching little kids, especially teaching them math or science or social studies! Plus, who can handle fifty little bur-heads on their own?" Molly shouted at him, not really wanting an answer.

"Well –"

She interrupted him before he could protest. "Plus, where are you going to get the materials for this? Teaching guides? Books for the kids? Paper, pencils, calculators, stuff like that, Burt? I can't just go off the cuff on this. They might actually remember what I teach them – not that I'm saying I'll do it – and what if it's wrong information? I can teach them about how politics impacted literature in the nineteenth century, not how to divide fractions!"

"Well, we thought we'd get materials from each other's stockpiles, and hoped maybe the kids and their parents could give you an idea of what they were learning right before the Blackout, and point you in the right direction."

"Seriously?" She eyed him. "That's all you're giving me to work with?"

He sputtered a bit. "Well, and of course we'd get someone to help you...manage the group."

She folded her arms over her chest and stared him down. "And who will mind the farm while I'm expanding young minds?"

"We'll figure it out. Don't worry about that part."

Molly sighed. "At this point, Burt, I think I'd prefer to stay on farm duty."

"I know. Just think about it, OK? Let me know when you've decided." He left her standing, hoe in hand, surrounded by knee-high corn stalks.

And that's how she became the town's teacher.

18.

On about day thirty-four after the Blackout, Gary made it deep into Virginia. He camped along an inlet off the Chesapeake Bay. In the seventeen days since he'd left D.C. he'd seen a handful of people, but he hadn't really had a conversation with anyone since Baltimore. He talked out loud, sang, whistled, anything just to feel like he wasn't alone.

It was nice there by the water's edge. The days were getting cold as November settled in. Gary didn't mind. He liked the cooler weather, and he had a nice coat and a few layers of clothing, even if they were pretty dingy. The air was crisp and clear with just a hint of salt in it.

He got out the map to study it. He'd had to cut across small portions of land lately, since the bay made the coast jagged and inefficient. Most of the time, it only took a day to cross, so he still had access to plenty of fish by the time he was ready to set up camp. The peninsula he was pondering wasn't much different than the others, and he figured he could cross it in a day, day and a half tops, but only if he got going.

Gary had walked about two hundred and seventy-five miles in thirty days. He was averaging just under ten miles a day.

Not bad, Gary supposed. *At my current rate, though, it will be another seventy days before I make it home to Molly.* He frowned. *Seventy days. Can I walk for another seventy days?* After logging nearly three hundred miles on his shoes, they weren't in the greatest shape. Not to mention his clothes. They were filthy, and even though he tried to wash them at every opportunity, fresh water was reserved for drinking, which meant clothes got washed in salt water, leaving them crusty and overall less than clean.

He sat on the banks of the bay and spotted a few dolphins playing about a hundred yards out. It really was a nice spot. He could stay there pretty easily. There was plenty of fish to go around and keep him well-fed. He could probably even find some nuts or berries in the dune grasses.

He studied the map a bit closer. He wasn't all that far from Colonial Williamsburg. He wondered how they were faring in all of this. He'd heard that in some parts of town, at least before the Blackout, they had blacksmiths, fully self-sustaining farms and lived like they did before the light bulb brought a wave of technology like the world had never seen.

Maybe I could offer some help in exchange for shelter and food, he thought.

He was so tired. The prospect of settling in, of reaching a place he could stay, was tempting.

The power will probably be on before my seventy days is up anyway, right? What's the point in nearly killing myself trying to get home, when surely the power will be restored soon?

Gary considered the possibility. Realistically, when the power came back, it was possible anarchy could reign. People might not know what to do. It was hard to know what was left of the government, with no word from them in over a month. How would they maintain control? It was possible it could be like providing a feast to a starving family. Would the people know what to do with what was spread before them? Would they consume it so fast that they would leave the host family with nothing? Or, would they hoard it, leaving nothing for others? Would they ration their supply, or would people simply pick up where they left off?

At the very least, he decided he should walk to Williamsburg. *Maybe I can re-supply there if I decide to continue on*, he thought.

It was a good seventy miles to Williamsburg, so he was looking at another week of walking at least.

He sighed and folded the map. "Well. No time like the present," he said aloud to the landscape. "Just put one foot in front of the other."

19.

The closest school was a few miles away. It was too far to walk to regularly, especially for the littler kids, but it was close enough to take supplies from. One of the guys even went and got a double-sided chalkboard on wheels to set up in the living room - what was now the main classroom. Before the school could open officially, they spent three days hauling supplies. Even Jimmy helped where he could, when he wasn't working on fine-tuning the town's defenses.

Then Christmas came. Despite all their troubles, there it was. So, they delayed the start of school. The holiday fell on a Saturday that year, so they decided to start classes the following Monday.

It was an odd Christmas. There were no festive lights, no typical gifts to speak of, nothing like that. However, Molly had an artificial tree that she got down from the attic and decorated with ornaments. It was dark, but pretty.

She even made Dug a gift out of some of Gary's old t-shirts. Heck, he wasn't using them right now anyway. It turned out to be a pretty crude-looking bear, but Dug loved it. He played with it all day and carried it to bed that night.

She spent the day lazing around, trying not to think about how other people were spending it, or how she should have been spending it with Gary, if he was lucky enough to be home for it.

In the evening, she lit some candles as it got darker, and treated herself to a glass of wine. She'd been saving the wine for who knows what, but it was Christmas, and she decided she was entitled to something special.

That night, much like the previous seventy nights, she said a silent prayer for Gary and hoped for a Christmas miracle, even if that miracle was just that he survived another day.

The first week of school was total chaos. The kids didn't know what to do, and neither did Molly. But they worked through the growing pains, and fell into a routine by about the third week. It had been almost three months since the Blackout, and they were coping. They all dreamed of life before, and when it would return to "normal", but no one really talked about it much anymore.

Beth McMiller, the woman Burt had guilted into helping out at the school, taught math and science and assisted Molly for other subjects. They ended up with about twenty-eight kids, and it was a lot of bodies to cram into Molly's house. On days when it was nice, she liked to have classes outside. Today was just such a day.

She had a few of the older boys carry the chalkboard to the backyard, and gathered the kids around it. The younger ones were clustered in groups of four or five, discussing their assigned reading while Beth floated between the groups. Molly was working with the older kids on Nathaniel Hawthorne's *The Scarlet Letter*. It was one of the books Molly could remember best from when she was in high school, so she thought it would be safe. They were nearly finished with the volume, and were really getting into the meat of the story.

"So, how do we feel about Hester's situation? Is it

fair? Did she bring it upon herself?" Molly asked the group.

Hands shot up. Tommy Dewater was the first to speak. "I'm not sure it's an issue of fair or not. It was the standard of the time. Adultery was a crime of the worst kind, so she was punished. It wouldn't be fair if there was another woman in the story who did the same thing and wasn't punished, but it's not like they kept the consequences of such actions a secret back then."

"OK Tommy. That's a good point. How about the flip side though? Along the same lines of fairness: Why is the woman punished and not the man? It takes two people to commit adultery. To me, it would seem the husband or wife who was cheated on should get to stone the man involved in the crime, or something. In fact, women were often viewed as less intelligent than men at that time. A crafty man could have lured an unsuspecting woman to stray from a loving marriage pretty easily, it would seem to me. What of that?" she asked.

"Well, that also seems typical of the time period, doesn't it?" A girl who was young for the group, named Sophie, chimed in. She had an irritated look on her face, and raised one dark eyebrow as she made her point. "I mean, look at *The Witch of Blackbird Pond*." They'd read that one first, and it was fairly well received. "That wasn't about a man being falsely accused of witchcraft and made to face death for something he didn't do. It was a woman. In fact, how many men were accused of witchcraft and burned or drowned for their crime, Mrs. Bonham?"

Molly smiled. She loved how passionate they were about it. Sometimes it was hard to get this kind of enthusiasm out of the college kids, so she anticipated more of a fight from the younger group. But they embraced the lessons with all the fervor she did, and she loved every minute of it.

"Not too many, Sophie, to be perfectly honest. I don't think it was unheard of, but it just didn't happen as widely as it did to women. Generally speaking, men were the leaders of the town, and although their wives and daughters may have manipulated and planted the seed, it was men who mostly did the public accusing."

Molly sat down in an empty space to complete the circle the kids had made in the grass in front of the chalkboard. "So, getting back to Hester, you're right, her treatment is fairly typical of her time period. How would she have coped if she had lived in today's world?"

"I think that depends," a blond-headed boy named Chase said.

"On what?" she asked.

"Whether she did it before the Blackout, or after."

Molly was puzzled. He said it so matter-of-factly, but she had no idea what difference the power outage made in terms of adultery. "Please, elaborate."

"Well, before the Blackout, it doesn't seem like it was that unusual for people to cheat. Adultery was a sort of archaic word, wasn't it? People just broke up and went their separate ways if their partner found out. No big deal. But the world has shrunk since the Blackout. Families are more important. People are working through their issues. I think adultery would be more of a major crime as our society circles round to be more similar to that of Hester's, don't you?"

"What do you mean by our society being more similar to Hester's, Chase?" Molly eyed him skeptically, curious and slightly fearful of the point he was trying to make.

"Well, just that. There are a lot of parallels now. More than there were eighty-five days ago, that's for sure. Like I said, our world is smaller now. We know each other's business. We have to work harder for our food, clothes, materials, everything really. We can relate more to the things Hester and the other characters went through, because we're going through those same things. If I get a hole in my shirt, I don't run over to Old Navy and buy another one. I bug my mom to sew it up, and eventually end up doing it myself when she's too busy."

They all laughed, and Chase went on. "Even our pacing has slowed to match Hester's. Hester could never fathom driving thirty miles to work, putting in eight hours, driving home, picking Pearl up from soccer practice on the way, fixing dinner, having family game night with Pearl, getting her to bed at a reasonable hour, then turning around and doing it all again the next day. Frankly, that's unrealistic for all of us today, whereas three months ago, it was the norm."

Molly glanced down at her wedding ring and thought of Gary. "So Chase, what do you think would happen if someone you knew was involved in an affair today?"

He thought for a moment. "Well, I don't think she'd be made to wear a letter A or anything, but if she was the guilty one, I think she'd lose a lot of friends, and essentially be an outcast." He paused. "A lot like Hester was. But I think that's the difference. If the guy was the guilty one, I think he'd face the same fate. Our society has evolved that much at least. Men aren't unconditionally innocent anymore." He looked around at the other boys in the group. "Unfortunately."

Everyone laughed again. "So, you better be on your best behavior, then!" Molly said. She stood up and brushed the grass from her shorts. "Alright, great work today! Let's read the next two chapters for tomorrow, OK?"

That night, she took some dinner over to Jimmy's house. She hadn't seen much of him lately, and missed him. She found herself needing him more than she probably should, but she couldn't help it. Without Gary, what else could she do?

Dug trotted happily beside her as they walked up his driveway. She balanced her canned-good casserole concoction in one hand and knocked on the door with the other.

"Hey, Molly. What's up?" Jimmy said through a partially opened door.

"Nothing. Wanna have dinner?" She offered her food.

"Oh. Sure. C'mon in." He opened the door wide to let her in, and scanned the street suspiciously before closing the door behind her.

"So, how's the Watch going?" Molly asked, collecting plates from where he pointed.

"It's..." he paused. "We're weak, Molly. And the Wanderers know it. At least a few of them do."

She looked up from distributing the silverware. "What do you mean by that?"

"Well, Burt doesn't want people to know, because he doesn't want to start a panic, but a group of Wanderers has been casing the place, making threatening movements, and just...I dunno, acting suspicious. I think they're up to something."

"Who are they?"

He looked at her, and she knew. *Craig.* "What does he want?"

They sat across from each other as he spooned some casserole onto his plate. "Who knows. Revenge? His home back? Food? Your guess is as good as mine.

But I'm pretty sure he has friends on the inside, so if he wants to do some damage, he will. It's simply a matter of when he will strike."

They sat in silence for a while after that, with Dug at Molly's feet, thumping his tail if she moved slightly. Molly quit asking him about the radio, hoping he'd speak up if it was important. But she couldn't help wondering as she sat in the same house with it.

Eventually, Jimmy cleared his throat. "So, tell me about this school they have you running."

She talked about it for a bit, telling him about the day's lesson and what Chase had said. She appreciated the distraction from the grim news he'd given her.

"One of my students tried to claim that we were living in a time very similar to that of Hester Prynne. Remember her? From *The Scarlet Letter*? Anyway, he made some valid points. Some that I wasn't too comfortable with."

Jimmy grunted. "Like what?"

"Oh, just that the world had shrunk, similar to the size it was then, and things had slowed down."

"I don't see anything upsetting about that. It's true."

"No, I know. But I don't really want to recede back to such a dark time of superstition and that 'accuse now and ask questions after the person is dead' kind of mentality, ya know?"

He chuckled. "I don't see what's funny about that," Molly said.

"It's just a bit dramatic, don't you think?"

"Obviously I don't."

"Well, don't you think we're more logical than we were then? That we have more information? Yes, our immediate world is smaller, but we know a larger world surrounds us. We have explanations for things like eclipses, not superstitions and angry gods. Don't you think that will improve the social situation some?"

"You're the one in charge of the town's defense. You tell me."

He frowned. "I protect the townspeople from outsiders, not each other."

They cleared the dishes in silence, and Molly helped him clean up. He walked her home that night, since it was after dark by the time they were done, all the time not speaking. Dug walked happily between the two of them, taking the occasional pat on the head.

They reached her driveway and he turned to her. "Well, thanks for dinner tonight, Molly. It was great."

"Sure. No problem." She hugged him, and he embraced her warmly. She pulled back and looked deep into his emerald eyes. "I hope you'll protect me from anything."

He opened his mouth to speak, but before he could she turned and went into her house.

20.

Forty-one days after the Blackout, Gary reached what was left of Colonial Williamsburg. Ashen remains were everywhere. There appeared to have been a riot, or some type of battle, and this was ground zero. It made him nervous.

It was so quiet, he could almost hear the ashes smoldering. He scoffed at himself. Obviously this mess was weeks old, probably the result of some irrational folks thinking they were more deserving of the supplies here than their neighbor.

The road crunched under his feet and the sound was oppressive. He tried to step lighter, but the ash blanketed everything.

What happened to the people who lived here? Were they killed? Did they run? He thought. He was just glad he wasn't there when anarchy reigned.

Gary scanned the horizon, debating what to do. Going further into town would probably yield more of the same. Any supplies that were there had either been destroyed or taken by now. He searched for a place to ponder the map, but there was nothing. No shelter. No safe place to sit. Nothing. He was nearing the end of his rope, hoping Williamsburg would offer some respite, but it appeared his rope just got longer.

He sighed and turned back. He couldn't stay there. He had to find someplace to re-group and just keep walking. The problems with his shoes and clothes would have to be solved another day. He might be barefoot and naked by the time he got home, but he had to find the way home sooner or later.

Gary turned back the way he came and walked to a small wooded area for some shelter before he stopped to study the map. He sat with his back to a pine tree, put his pack in his lap, and rested his unfolded map on top of it. He resisted the urge to crumple or maim it. Every time he looked at the damn thing the distance between point A and point B didn't seem to shrink much, no matter how far he walked. But it was his only lifeline.

He took a deep breath and resolved to be constructive. In the coming weeks, he would have to make a choice – continue following the coast, with a solid food source, or cut the travel time and veer inland a bit. Gary hated to extend his journey, but abandoning a known food source made him nervous. He didn't have anything useful to kill game with, if there was even any to be had. He also didn't have any salt or anything to preserve fish with, eliminating the possibility of storing up food before he veered away from the coast.

He considered the map. At the furthest point from the water, he'd be sixty miles or so from food.

That's too far to walk if I was starving. I'd have to decide quickly to turn towards the coast if it became necessary. But it's always an option. If I don't find food in the first day or two, I could always turn east, he thought.

One nice thing about walking the coast was that there weren't too many big cities, so he avoided most of the Wanderers. Venturing inland might put him in unnecessary danger. Molly would never know he was making good time if he was killed before he got home.

Gary decided a middle-of-the-road approach was best. Most of the bays had feeder rivers that went a little ways inland, and he could travel between them without too much extra time. If he took 64 to 664, he could find food in the wildlife refuge. He didn't want to cut across it, for fear of getting lost inside, but if he skirted the west side of it, he could be at one of the many rivers in another day's walk. More of the same awaited him further south.

He had at least sixty-three days before he would be home. Sixty-three more days of walking. Sixty-three more days of surviving. Sixty-three more days without Molly.

It was a long time.

The Storm
21.

"Into each life, some rain must fall."
– Henry Wadsworth Longfellow

A storm was coming. A storm that would stir the souls of the lives it touched. A storm with the potential to destroy what was left of the world as they knew it- a world they desperately struggled to hold on to.

22.

Beth and Molly were sitting on the back porch working on the week's lesson plans when a man came strolling around the side of the house. He was very striking and Molly had a hard time not staring. He had olive-colored skin and dark hair that shined in the sun. His button-down shirt was open at the top and untucked from his jeans, giving him a sexy, rumpled appearance.

"Hey. When are you coming home? You know Mom doesn't want you out past dark."

Confused, Molly realized he was talking to Beth. "I just want to finish up here. I'll be home before dark. Don't worry." There was a hint of annoyance in her voice.

He wandered up next to Beth and jammed his hands in his pockets. "Hey," he said and nodded in Molly's general direction.

"Hi."

"Oh. Molly, this is my brother, Seth. Seth, Molly."

Now that she knew it, she could see the similarities between the two of them. Beth had the same skin tone, slightly lighter hair, and the same shape to her face and eyes. "Nice to meet you," she said. He nodded again in response.

Beth sighed as an awkward silence descended. "I promise I'll have her home on time," Molly said through a smile. She nearly added 'sir' to the comment, but stopped herself. She didn't know if he could take a joke.

He cracked a bit of a smile. "You just better, or she'll be grounded."

"Alright. I'm sitting right here. And I'll get this done a lot faster if you leave us alone, Seth."

He chuckled and turned Molly's way again. Her heart fluttered a bit to have his beautiful brown eyes settled on her. "See ya round," he said with a distinct look of mischief in his eye.

"Sure," was all she could muster. *Idiot*, she thought as she watched him walk away. *You're acting like a teenager! You're married! Get a hold of yourself.*

"Sorry about that little…interruption," Beth said.

"No worries." She paused. "So, is he older or younger than you?"

"Younger, but only by two years. When the Blackout happened, my mom wanted us all in one place, so we moved back in. Neither one of us had gotten married yet or even been seeing anyone seriously, so it wasn't like we had to uproot families or anything. And lucky for her, we'd stayed close by."

Molly thought of her parents, who'd moved a thousand miles away before they both passed on. For the first time since they'd died, she was grateful they weren't around. She wasn't sure if she could handle worrying about Gary and the two of them – not knowing if they were OK, if they had enough food, if they'd been attacked by Wanderers. She returned her thoughts to Beth. She was in her mid-twenties, so that made her brother early twenties. He wasn't that much younger than Molly; only about a decade.

"Well, that worked out well."

"Yeah, it did for my mom." Beth chuckled a little. "She kind of drives us crazy with worrying. Especially after we were both used to having so much independence."

Molly couldn't imagine going back to living with her parents at this point, and being subject to curfews and rules again, so she sympathized. However, she couldn't help thinking that it must've been nice to have someone so close to worry about you. Realistically, it was scary out, and her mom's worries weren't overly unfounded.

"I feel for you, but it's dangerous out. You can't blame your mom for worrying."

She sighed. "I guess. I just…" She thought for a moment. "I never expected this is what my life would be. I had such ideas, ya' know? Dreams for myself, for my life." She chuckled a bit. "Let me tell you, they did *not* include living at home with my mother and brother at twenty-eight years old."

Molly frowned and nodded. She could say the same thing – the dreams she had for her life hadn't included living alone, not knowing whether her husband was dead or alive, and teaching at a K-through-whatever school.

"Well, we've all had to shift our focus, for lack of a better term. It's not been easy for anyone. And I s'pose we're all hoping this is temporary. I know I am. In fact, I'm not really hoping, I'm more…expecting. This isn't life as I know it, and the old way will come back eventually." Molly nodded to emphasize her point.

Beth looked across the yard, watching the wildflowers bend in the breeze. "Wouldn't you say the old way *has* come back?"

Molly couldn't get Beth's comment out of her head, so she decided to face it head on. She'd been debating about reading *Alas, Babylon* with the group for a few weeks. Worried the kids might panic about the subject matter, she considered skipping it. But the relevancy of it was too tempting, and her conversation with Beth tipped the scale.

The book took place in Fort Repose, a town in Central

Florida. Molly was never sure if it was a real town or not. It wasn't someplace she'd ever heard of, and she couldn't really go online and look it up. But the fact that it was in Florida hit home for all the kids.

The book received mixed reviews. Some of the kids simply didn't like it. Molly thought that was because it was too real, too much like what was happening. Others thought it was great, citing how innovative it was for the nineteen-fifties.

That day, they were seated outside in the grass, taking advantage of the beautiful December weather. "Now, I want to talk about some of the struggles the people in Frank's book faced, versus the ones we are facing," Molly suggested.

"Do you think we'll run out of salt?" One of the boys at the edge of the group asked.

"It's hard to say, Lewis. I hope not. And I don't even know if Frank's research on the effects of salt deficiency is sound." She thought about the people on the other side of the wall. "Right now, I think we have bigger problems."

"How come the people in Frank's book didn't have to deal with Wanderers?" Another asked.

"Well, it's hard to say. I think a lot of the other people were killed in the blasts, don't you? So they didn't really have an extraneous population wandering around looking for resources like we do. Ours was a catastrophic event, but not deadly." She thought of Gary, hoping that was true.

Cassandra piped up. She was a bright student, about sixteen years old. Her parents had been major supporters of Burt and the wall. "I don't think their struggles were all that different than ours, and I think the book is a testament to what we all have to look forward to." Silence fell heavily upon the group.

Bingo, Molly thought. It was what she was waiting for. Either she'd have a good discussion, or she'd crash and burn, and she was about to find out which.

"What makes you say that, Cassandra?" Molly asked.

"Well, look at them, and look at us. We've started farming, we've learned to like eating fish regularly, we've come together as a community, we've dug wells, and I think as supplies get more scarce, they'll also be more valuable. I mean, no one uses money anymore, or even speaks of it. All of our money was digital and disappeared with the power. Just like in Frank's book, food and supplies will become the unit of trade. You just watch."

Molly smiled. It was something she had considered as well. Jimmy had told her as much. Even in the early days, he knew.

"Well, having read this, what do you think you could suggest to Burt or the town leaders to help make our lives easier? What can we learn from the successes and mistakes of Frank's characters?"

No one had anything to offer, so Molly tried to start them off. "Ok, well, couldn't you argue that most of their struggles were from external sources? Food shortages, radiation poisoning, crime, things like that?"

Heads bobbed in agreement. "Well, some of our struggles have been internal. A selfish few planted a seed of doubt that grew into a small rebellion. Now, our town is a bit smaller."

"Yeah, well, now we have less people to care for, less to come up with supplies for," a boy in front snidely added.

"True. But my question is, why wouldn't Frank's characters rebel against each other the way we did?"

A quiet girl who never usually said much made eye contact with Molly. "Emma. Do you have something to add?"

"I just think that maybe Frank's book is a little optimistic. Maybe it was Frank's way of saying what he thought humanity should be like, not necessarily what it really is like." She paused. "I mean, in a crisis situation, you always want to believe people will help each other, that the best will come out, don't you think?"

Molly smiled. "Yes, Em. I do think."

Molly learned about the goodness of humanity that night. The attack came swiftly and quietly. Burt and his family were sleeping, but Jimmy was on duty at the wall and saw some movement. By the time he tracked the intruders down, they were at Burt's house, setting it aflame. They were standing in the shadows when Jimmy and his team tackled them, and a group of neighbors worked to get the small fire out.

Burt burst from his home demanding an explanation. Jimmy held the leader from behind while he squirmed and thrashed, trying to get free.

He grasped the man's face and turned it into the light. He was bearded, dirty, and wild, but recognizable. "Craig."

The people watching the scene gasped in unison.

"I suppose it was your brood that set the supplies on fire too?"

He responded by spitting in Burt's face. There were four other men being restrained as well, but they weren't fighting like Craig was.

Burt sighed. "This cannot be tolerated. I sentence all five of you to death. You will be executed immediately. Jimmy, lead them to the square. I'll be there shortly."

Jimmy nodded, while the crowd watched in disbelief.

Death? Molly thought. She ran to Burt as he went back into his house. "Burt! Death? Are you sure about this?"

"Molly, for heaven's sake, not now."

"But you have kids, Burt! Can you really kill five men?"

He went to his gun cabinet and pulled out a 9mm handgun. "I can, and will. Molly, I'm a cop. I've done it before." He turned to face her. "They would've killed me and my family today. And the attacks won't quit until I stop them."

Molly knew he was right, but how could he live with himself after killing five people?

"Maybe you can keep them prisoner and put them to work? The town can always use laborers."

He unlocked the cabinet where he kept the ammo. "The town doesn't need more mouths to feed, particularly ungrateful ones."

Molly watched him load the weapon and walk out the front door. He'd made his decision, and Molly wasn't sure she wanted to watch him go through with it.

She went to the porch and saw Jimmy waiting with the prisoners. He made eye contact with her, but his stare was emotionless. She lowered her gaze and turned to go back inside.

Burt's family sat around their kitchen table, heads bowed, hands held. *Praying for what?* Molly wondered. *For the souls of the men their father was about to dispatch? For their father to have the strength he needs? For themselves? For the town?*

She leaned against the doorframe, watching them. *Who needs it most?*

23.

It had been five days since Gary left Williamsburg. He was on the west side of 664, debating walking over to the Naval Reserve and seeing what was up. After what happened in D.C., he wasn't sure of the reception he would receive. He wasn't sure it was worth the risk. He would probably be better off going around it, although he risked missing out on valuable supplies and information. Decided, he started to pack up when a sound startled him. He fumbled for the Leatherman. A group of scruffy men came out of the brush, dangling various weapons from their hands. One had what looked like a broom handle, one had a hammer, one had a sharpened triangle of metal that might have come off of just about anything. Only one of them had a genuine weapon, a knife - a fairly large one at that, one you might use to skin a deer.

Gary held the Leatherman in his left hand loosely, not to be too threatening, but to demonstrate that he wasn't going down without a fight. "Can I help you with something, fellas?"

"Looks like you've got a pretty nice setup here." The man with the knife eyed Gary's fire, the map spread out next to it, the pack on his back and his coat.

"Can't complain."

"Maybe you'd like to share with those..." he glanced at the men on either side of him and grinned, "a little less fortunate than you." The other men laughed.

"I don't have any more food, fellas. You can check my pack. I caught the fish I ate this morning in the river. Sorry. I don't have much to share." He bent over and picked up the map and began folding it.

The man with the knife let out a single chuckle. "You misunderstood what I meant by share. See, we want what you've got. And we tend to get what we want."

They moved in on him slowly from all sides. Gary could tell they meant to kill him, over a Leatherman, a map, a backpack, and some fishing line. That was what the value of his life was, apparently.

He wasn't going down without a fight.

It became clear rather quickly that they'd done this before. They had a system. Intimidate, frighten, fight, kill. That was their process. Frankly, they were doing a good job with it. Fear threatened to choke Gary as they closed in. The man with the broom handle held it in his left hand and smacked his right with it. The man with the sharpened metal smiled menacingly. The man with the hammer choked up on the handle and narrowed his eyes. He considered Gary a task that needed doing. The others enjoyed it.

They didn't come at him all at once. It was a matter of entertainment, not efficiency. The man with the broom handle went first. He was strong, but not terribly coordinated. Gary blocked his attack easily and stabbed him with the knife in the Leatherman. He recoiled and Gary turned to face the guy with the metal. Gary didn't think he could really stab with it. He'd have to slash, and hit something major, like the neck, to do any real damage. So, Gary tried to tire him out. He let the man wave wildly, missing, mostly. He got Gary once in the arm, and once across the back, but with all the adrenaline pumping, Gary didn't feel it much.

After one poorly timed slash, Gary was able to grab the man's wrist and stab him hard in the stomach. He wretched much the same way the man with the broom handle had, and slumped away.

The man with the knife sighed impatiently. "Enough of this. Lou, finish up here, would ya? I have other things to do today." A smile crossed his face as he looked at Gary. "Like fish."

Lou circled Gary a bit before he moved in. Gary was at the disadvantage. Lou had watched Gary fight the first two; he knew his strengths and weaknesses, knew he was getting tired, that the adrenaline was wearing off. Gary looked wildly from Lou's face to his hammer, trying to anticipate what he might do.

To his credit, he didn't drag it out. He circled, and Gary became impatient, so he slashed his knife at the man. He seized the opportunity and drove his hammer into Gary's back, knocking him to the ground, but not unconscious. The backpack offered little protection, as it was mostly empty by that point. The pain was unimaginable. It consumed Gary. He thought he might be sick.

But Lou wasn't done. He kicked Gary's ribs, stomach, and back. Gary curled into a ball, trying to protect himself, but then Lou turned the hammer on Gary's legs and arms. Gary could taste blood before he started to lose consciousness.

He heard the man with the knife approach. "Good work, Lou. Now, let's see if he was worth all that trouble, hmm?"

He didn't hear Lou's response before he blacked out.

When Gary woke up it was dark. He shivered. He looked down to discover he was naked, save for boxer shorts. He turned to see where he was, but the pain that resulted consumed him, and he blacked out again.

Eventually, Gary managed to crawl over to an area shaded by bushes. He was cold, hungry and thirsty. But he was so immobile he knew there wasn't much he could do about it.

What happened? He wondered before drifting off. Whether it was sleep or just unconsciousness, Gary didn't care. All he knew was, he was delivered from the hell that had suddenly become his life.

A big man with red hair and simple clothes to match his simple life spotted him. He was on his way back home when he saw an arm, palm side up, sticking out of the brush in the dunes.

"Hey!" He shouted. "Hey! You OK?"

The lifeless form didn't respond. Judd rushed over and half crashed into him and half knelt down beside him, trying to shake some life into him. "Hey, come on now, you answer me."

By the look of him, he'd been roughed up pretty good. Angry purple bruises spotted his chest, sides and face. Looked to Judd like at least one of the poor man's arms was broken.

He leaned down and put his ear next to Gary's nose and discovered he was still breathing.

Resolved, he slung Gary over his shoulder and carried him home.

Judd lived with his mother and father on a large farm. He burst through the back door with Gary over his shoulder.

His mom, Julia, was working in the kitchen. "My goodness, Judd. Is that racket really necessary." She wiped her hands on her apron as she turned around. "What's happened?"

"Not sure. He needs some help."

"Well don't just stand there with the poor boy slung over yo shoulder like a sack o' potatoes. Take him upstairs! I'll be there with some water and rags shortly."

"Henry! We got some trouble in here!" She hollered out the back window, hoping her husband was close enough to hear her.

She rushed upstairs, not spilling a single drop of hot water along the way. She set the pot of water on the nightstand next to the bed and soaked the first rag. As she rung it out, she looked Gary over while Judd stood on the other side of the bed.

"My my. Someone really worked him over."

"What's happened?" Henry asked.

"Oh, I didn't see you come in, Henry. Judd's brought us a boy that's been beaten pretty badly."

"Whaddya think?"

"I think we best help him any way we can."

He nodded. "Anything I can do?"

"Just stay outta my way for now."

He grunted and turned to leave. He clapped Judd on the shoulder on the way out. "Ya done the right thing, bringin' him here."

Judd nodded and watched his father go back to work.

Gary woke up forty-eight hours after arriving on Judd's farm. Julia was sitting in the chair next to his bed mending a shirt that belonged to one of the boys.

He groaned. Everything hurt.

"Well now, good morning to you." Julia said. She set her sewing down on the nightstand and leaned closer. She smelled like cinnamon. It was very soothing to him.

"What's your name, child?"

"Ga..." he croaked. His voice was raw from lack of use, or trauma, he wasn't sure which. He cleared his throat. "Gary."

Julia handed him a cup of water. "Nice to meetcha Gary. I'm Julia. My son Judd found ya two days ago over by the river. What were ya doin' out there in nothing but your skivvies?"

His mind was foggy. He remembered being cold, and hurt. He remembered thinking he was going to die. But he couldn't put his finger on why he'd been there in the first place.

"I...I'm not sure."

"Can ya tell me where you're from? Where do ya live, honey? You got family worrin' about ya?"

Gary's eyebrows came together. He shook his head. "I don't know."

"Well, don't you worry. I'm sure it'll all come back to ya. In the meantime, you just rest. When you're feelin' better, you can help Judd out on the farm."

He nodded. She stood to leave and put her hand on his forehead. "Don't trouble yourself. It'll all work out in its own time."

Gary found little comfort in her words as he lay in a strange bed, in a strange place, full of strangers; including him.

Instead of pressuring Gary, they allowed him to rest, heal and eventually settle into a routine. He was hurt pretty bad, but without the aid of X-rays and other modern technologies, it was difficult to tell how extensive the damage was.

In the beginning, small things had been milestones, like getting out of bed or getting dressed. It took over a week for him to come downstairs and eat with them. After that, he spent as much time as he could outside exploring the land, and every day he got a little further. Their land was huge. Acres and acres of fields with all types of crops, that kept them fed. Despite the fact that winter was closing in fast, Judd explained they'd always had something to eat, and something to take care of. They even shared with the neighbors who were willing to come get it.

Henry was a down-to-earth man in his mid-sixties. He was thin as a rail with a white curly beard. He always wore overalls and a baseball cap to keep the sun out of his face. One day, Gary asked him about the food sharing, and he said, "Well, I've got enough to go round here, but I can't be going all over creation takin' food. But if they're willin' to come get it, they can have what they can carry."

In fact, they had so much to go around, Judd's father said they hadn't had trouble with the type folks were calling "Wanderers." Apparently they were thieves with no home to call their own. They just roamed around, violently taking from those who worked for what they had. But Judd's family always had enough, and gave willingly, so they hadn't seen much hostility from Wanderers. And if the Wanderers started feeling a sense of entitlement, Judd and his dad had no trouble "straightening them out," whatever that meant.

The home they shared was huge, and Gary wondered how Julia kept it up. She was a small woman, also in her mid-sixties, built from a life of working with her hands. She didn't take 'nothin' from nobody', but she was sweet as the pies she made. She often told stories about her life growing up in Virginia, about Judd when he was a kid, and how she met his father. By the time Gary was ready to start helping out, he felt like he knew her whole life history.

Eventually they gave Gary chores to do around the farm, and he liked it. It was quiet. No sense of urgency, except for this tiny part of him that tugged at the back of his mind. Like he was supposed to be somewhere, with someone. Usually he just ignored it.

One day, about a month after Gary arrived at their farm, he was bringing in an armload of chopped wood. Despite the chill in the air, he was sweating from swinging the ax. He piled the wood next to the stove and stood to wipe his forehead with his sleeve. He smiled down at the pile, pleased. He was achingly sore, but a few weeks ago, it would've been too much to manage, so he considered the pain a good thing.

Julia smiled at him. "That's mighty fine." She looked at Gary, and he could tell she had more coming. So he waited for her to get there. "Honey, we love havin' you here. You been a big help round here. But don't you wanna know who you are? What if your family is worrin' 'bout you?"

Gary sat down heavily at the kitchen table. "Yes, of course I want to know who I am. But how am I supposed to find out?"

She plopped a loaf of bread and a jar of homemade strawberry jam in front of him. "I don't know, but you best think on it. You could stay here forever, but do you really want to?"

24.

Things were different after the executions. It was quieter. Movements were more stilted, people were more leery. Molly wasn't sure it was a change for the better. Jimmy hadn't said much to her about it, and she hadn't asked. She wasn't sure she even wanted to know anything more. She simply tried to do her best to live her life the best way she knew how. But she found even that was difficult anymore.

It had been ninety days since the Blackout. Ninety. Three months without contact from Gary. Molly was feeling the loss especially heavily that day, for some reason. She was grouchy and depressed all day. When she was alone, she found herself tearing up, and when she was with poor Beth, she snapped rudely at her. Molly didn't host a lively literature discussion that day. Instead she had them quietly writing their thoughts so she could dwell on her depression.

She was sitting at the kitchen table when Beth found her at the end of the day. She sat down across from Molly.

"*What* is wrong?" she asked, exasperated.

"Nothing," Molly said, not taking her eyes off her paperwork.

"You're acting like a total bitch. I can tell something is wrong."

Molly finally looked up to find her staring intently, more concern than irritation on her face.

Molly sighed. "I don't know what's wrong, Beth. I'm just upset today. It's been ninety days since I've heard from Gary, and I'm just sick of being lonely and worried and just...not knowing!"

The words 'not knowing' echoed around the kitchen. She hadn't even realized she'd raised her voice. Beth sat back in the chair and folded her arms over her chest.

"Sorry," Molly said.

"Why? Sorry for what? For having emotions? For feeling cheated in all of this? For wanting this to be over? What?"

"No, I guess I'm not sorry for any of those things."

Beth smiled with one side of her mouth. "Listen, why don't you come over tonight and have dinner with us? It'll be fun!"

"I'm not sure you want my grey cloud of depression hanging over your dinner table."

"Sure we do!" she said enthusiastically, and Molly chuckled a little. "Come on! Now we'll have a fourth to play Cranium! I'll let you be on Seth's team."

Molly panicked internally. "What makes you think I would want to be on his team?"

"He's only the best Cranium player ever. He's unbeatable! If you're with him, you're guaranteed to win."

Whew. "Well, I guess it could be fun."

Beth got up and pushed her chair under the table. "Darn right. We eat at six. See you then!"

"Wait! What can I bring?" Molly didn't want to be a burden on their food supply. She had her own rations she could provide.

"Nothing but your smiling face." Beth called as she walked out.

"See ya," Molly quietly called after her. She sat back in

her chair, replaying the events in her head. She supposed it might be time to make friends with people her own age. Jimmy was great, but she viewed him as more of a father figure than a friend. It was past time to do something halfway normal – go have dinner with friends! Seeing Seth there was a bit of a bonus.

I mean, what could it hurt just to look at him? Guilt washed over her. *How would I feel if Gary was ogling another woman, thinking 'what could it hurt just to look'?* Molly considered cancelling, but that would require walking over there to tell them she wasn't coming. She steeled herself against Beth's handsome brother and tried to mentally prepare herself for a long night.

That night, Molly took a deep breath and knocked on the door to the McMiller residence. She'd dressed in a pink button-down blouse and jeans. No need to look like she was trying too hard.

Beth's mom answered the door. "Hello dear! How are you?" Before Molly could answer, she said, "Come in, come in! I've got a few things simmering on the stove, and the kids are in the living room." Mrs. McMiller was one of the few people in town who had a gas stove, and because of the way she'd rationed, she was the only one in town with gas left, except of course for Jimmy.

"Thank you, Mrs. McMiller. Can I help you with anything?"

"Oh no! Go on and visit with the kids. Dinner'll be along shortly. We're having our pork rations tonight!"

The town's farm had become fairly sustainable, but only because of the rationing efforts of Burt and the others in charge. Hoarding and gorging were strictly prohibited, so everyone had just enough to stay fed and healthy. But they only got to have some kind of meat about once a week, unless they went and caught fish themselves, so Molly knew the pork was special.

"Well thank you for including me! I can't wait to taste

it!"

Mrs. McMiller waved a hand over her shoulder as she walked toward the kitchen, and Molly headed for the living room.

The room was typically decorated for the area: a floral pattern covered the walls to the chair rail, then changed to a light grey color down to the floors. Antique-style furniture in coordinating colors was scattered throughout. There was a fireplace in the corner, and a dusty, useless TV hung above it. Beth and Seth were playing cards when Molly walked in.

Seth had his back to her, so Beth saw her first. "Oh, hey Molly! I'm glad you decided to come!" She put her cards down and stood to greet Molly. Seth followed suit.

"Good to see you again," he said as he looked straight into Molly's eyes. She felt like he could read her betraying thoughts, so she tried to hide her blush by turning to Beth.

"So, whatcha playin?"

"Nerds. Wanna join? We can start over."

"Of course, when I was beating you for once!" Beth complained.

"No, that's fine. Finish up. I'll learn your strategies so I can cream you both after dinner."

They laughed and quickly finished their game, which left Seth victorious after quite a remarkable comeback, much to Beth's disappointment. It was good timing, because just as they were separating the cards, Mrs. McMiller called for dinner.

Seth was the perfect gentleman, helping his mother carry food to the table while Beth got drinks for everyone. For Molly, it was like being part of a family again. She sat in her chair watching everyone bustle around with their assigned tasks and relished that, even if only for a moment, she could be a part of this.

Conversation flowed easily between the four of them during dinner. Molly learned that Seth was a laborer for the town, maintaining the wall and helping folks fix things in their homes – basically a handyman for the eighteenth century. He had been a mechanic prior to the Blackout, so he had some trouble transitioning to general fix-it work, but he said he'd learned a lot in the last three months, and continued to learn how to use the tools available for tasks they weren't built for. Molly thought that was something they all had learned to do in the last three months.

Lord knows I'm not built to be teaching anyone younger than eighteen! Molly thought.

Beth had been working on her PhD in Mathematics when the Blackout happened. She'd wanted to be a mathematician. Although she was putting her knowledge to good use, it wasn't anywhere near what she'd intended to do. She'd dreamed of having her own office with white boards and numbers everywhere, solving the world's problems and discovering new numbers. She never thought teaching fractions to small children was in her future.

"Once the power comes back on, I want to move to New York and study with Derek Houser. He's really up and coming in the field." She paused. "At least he was before the Blackout." It was the first they'd talked about something like this out loud since the first week.

"What will you do, Molly?" Seth asked.

She thought for a moment. *My life is so different now. What will I do when the power comes back on?*

"Once the power comes back, the first thing I plan to do is get a hold of Gary. Find out where he is and what happened, and figure out how to get him home."

Mrs. McMiller looked sympathetically at her. "I can't imagine worrying about my husband like that for all this time. It's almost like you can't live your life. I mean, if you knew he was alive and just fine, you could move forward knowing you'd be reunited soon. If he wasn't, well you could move on, as difficult as that might be."

"Soon is sort of a nasty word anymore, isn't it?" Molly asked her plate while she pushed her green beans away from the mashed potatoes. She looked up at the happy family seated at the table with her. "He'll be home 'soon.' The power will be back 'soon.' You'll be safe 'soon.' What does that even mean? It's become an empty promise." Suddenly she wasn't very hungry, and she set her fork down.

Mrs. McMillan smiled. "My my, that's rather dark, isn't it, dear? I think 'soon' is a sign of hope. The promise that before long, you'll get what you need. And if you don't, you didn't need it as much as you thought you did. Never forget dear, you won't be left wanting if you know where to keep your faith."

"Huh," she said. It was all she could muster. Her eyes shimmered with all the broken promises that had been laid at her feet in the last ninety days.

Seth cleared his throat. "Well, I don't know about anyone else, but I'm looking forward to that dessert, Mom."

"Yes, well, you'll have to wait until the dishes have been cleared! If you're so excited about it, why don't you get started?"

Molly gave Seth a grateful glance, thanking him for changing the subject. He smiled in return.

The pie was fantastic, complete with some decadent whipped cream. Milk was so scarce and spoiled so quickly without proper refrigeration, it was seldom used for anything but drinking and mixing into foods. It was never used for treats anymore. But Molly was so glad Mrs. McMiller had chosen to splurge. The cream was heaven in her mouth. It was light and sweet and everything she had taken for granted ninety-one days ago.

They finished the evening with a game of Cranium by candlelight. As Beth promised, Molly got to be on Seth's team, and they won by a landslide. Beth proposed a second game and a partner change-up, but Mrs. McMiller said she was tired and wanted to go to bed. So Molly thanked her for a lovely meal and evening and off she went, but not before doling out orders.

From the top of the stairs she hollered down. "Seth, don't you make Molly walk home alone in the dark. You be a gentleman and make sure she gets home safe, you hear me?"

"Yes, Mom." Then he turned to Molly and gave her that look - the one that made her feel like he was looking at her soul- before shouting back up the stairs. "Don't worry. I'd never let anything happen to her."

They walked quietly in the darkness at first, a casual distance apart. They weren't out of reach of each other, but they weren't close enough to bump by accident either.

Beth had abandoned Molly, claiming she was too tired and wanted to go to bed. *Coward,* Molly thought, but then wondered who she was directing it at.

Seth took a deep breath and let it out again as sort of an *aaaahhh* sound. "It's a nice night."

"Yes. It's that time of year."

"It's about time. I was sick of sweating my tail off at night."

"Mmm," was all Molly could think to say to that. She wasn't sure she could handle visualizing Seth's sweaty 'tail' at that moment.

He jammed his hands in his pockets and walked, kicking small rocks in front of him. "I know you're friends with Beth and everything, but if you ever need someone to talk to or whatever, you can always…I almost said call me, but you can't really do that, can ya?"

"Nope. Not really." She realized too late that he'd gone out on a limb there and she left him hanging a little bit. "But thanks for the offer, I'll keep it in mind." *Idiot,* she thought.

They rounded Molly's street and her little house was barely visible in the moonlight, tucked between her neighbors. "You know, I've always loved your house, even when we were kids. I thought it was the coolest one," Seth said.

"What? That's not true. Why on Earth would a small boy pay any attention to one house over another?"

A mischievous smile crept across his face. "Probably because yours was the one we always said was haunted."

Molly raised her right eyebrow. "Huh."

"Yup. Old Man Kratchet lived there, and used to collect kids. They say his soul remains to torture the kids that are foolish enough to come too close to the house."

"Old Man Kratchet? Like, Bob Kratchet, from *The Christmas Carol*? Couldn't you be a little more original than that?"

"Hey, the Kratchet name is not exclusive to that story! It's true. I'm surprised you haven't seen him in all the years you've been living there."

They walked up her porch steps and she turned to him. "Somehow, I don't think I'll lose sleep tonight."

He put his hand on the door jam and leaned over her. "Well, if you do, you know who to call, so to speak." He brought his face mere inches from hers. She could smell his breath; remnants of pie filled her senses. He leaned in even closer, and Molly started to panic.

He's going to kiss me! The emotions battling in her mind left her frozen, reacting neither proactively or reactively. Her desire for the kiss shocked and horrified her. Her insides were in turmoil as he inched closer and closer.

"WATCH OUT!" he shouted.

Molly wasn't as much of a screamer as she was a gasper. She sucked in a huge amount of air and leapt into his arms faster than he could blink. He had quick reflexes and caught her easily, however his laughter disabled the use of his legs and he fell flat on his butt. They sat in a heap on the floor, tears streaming down his face, anger written across Molly's.

She sprang up, leaving him clutching his middle and trying to get his breath. "You should've seen your face." At which point, he made a terrible attempt at recreating her expression mere moments before.

She brushed the front of her shirt and pants off for no other reason than to have something to do. "Yes, well, we'll see who Bob Kratchet haunts tonight."

Seth's eyes sparkled. "I never said his first name was Bob."

Molly opened the front door and stepped inside. "Well, maybe I know him better than you think." She closed the door on him, leaving him standing on her front porch.

25.

She came to Gary in a dream. He stood in a garden, surrounded by hundreds of flowers. They were white, strung together and draped from the trees all around them, creating a magical atmosphere.

She walked towards him in a white dress, with something sparkling in her dark hair. The dress hugged her delicate curves, but was also modest and classy. It was perfect.

As she came towards him, he had a feeling they weren't alone, but he could only see her.

She was small but beautiful, with olive-toned skin and dark eyes. In that moment, she was everything he needed.

He woke up confused and excited all at once. *Was she real, or just someone I created?*

He lay awake the rest of the night thinking about her. Picturing her eyes, so dark you couldn't see where the color stopped and the iris began. Dreaming about touching her silky hair. Imagining what her kiss would be like. Wondering who she was.

In the morning, he mentioned the dream to Julia. He was out of his mind about it, but he tried to act casual. "So, I had a dream last night about a woman, what do you make of that?"

She smacked the flour from her apron and said sternly, "I don't need no details 'bout some dream 'tween you and a woman."

Gary turned six shades of red and cleared his throat. "Not that kind of dream, Julia. I think it was a wedding." He paused. "My wedding."

She sat in the chair across from Gary and snatched a biscuit out from the bread basket. "Well, let's hear 'bout it then."

She sipped her tea and he tried to sort it out. "Well, there wasn't much to it. Just her. I could see her clear as day. And she was so... beautiful. Mesmerizing, really." He hesitated. "In fact, I can't stop thinking about her."

"Isn't that something? It's funny how yo' mind works yo' problems in the night." She chuckled to herself as she got up from the table, sipping her tea.

"Well, what do you make of it?"

"I think the better question is, what do *you* make of it?"

"Do you think she's real?"

"I 'reckon she might be. Or, she could just be somethin' yo' mind made up when you's thinkin' 'bout how lovely I am." She laughed at herself and swatted Gary with a towel. "Now, quit hangin' around my kitchen and get to work."

Gary thought about the woman in white all day while he was helping Judd tend the animals in the barn. Judd had to get his attention more than once to keep him from getting kicked.

"What's with you today?" he asked when they were finishing up.

After the less than helpful chat with his mother, Gary wasn't quite ready to discuss the mystery woman again. "Nothing. Just distracted I guess. Sorry. I'll try to be more focused tomorrow."

"Well, you just better. We're working with the big machines tomorrow, and you've got to be on your game with that stuff or someone can get hurt."

"I know."

He smiled and clapped his hand on Gary's shoulder. "Come on. Let's go see what Momma's got cookin'."

After a hearty meal, Gary lay awake thinking about her. She haunted him. It was ridiculous. Almost like he was in love with her – with a woman he dreamed up.

A thought occurred to him, and he sat up in bed. "She's my wife," he whispered to the darkness.

26.

Molly lay awake that night thinking about the men in her life. It was ridiculous. Seth wasn't really *in* her life. He was barely a friend. He was her co-worker's sibling. He'd been a nice guy and walked her home last night. They had an easy conversation, he played a typical boy's practical joke, and that was it. The infatuation she'd recently developed for him was nothing more than the void left by Gary's complete and total absence needing to be filled.

If Gary had developed a similar infatuation – because of course, that's all it was – Molly would have to learn to be understanding. She realized she was clenching her teeth, and it was starting to give her a headache. She took a deep breath and was trying to relax when a terrifying thought hit.

What if he's decided to stay with her? What if he's made a life with her, and isn't trying to come back here? What if he is alive, but has chosen not to come home? The thought was worse than thinking he'd died, and she allowed herself to wallow in it for only a moment. Something like that was completely out of character for Gary. He was devoted to her, to them, to the life they'd built. If he was alive, he was working to come home. Molly knew it.

Yet, Molly was totally devoted to Gary, too, but she had allowed this seed into her life - a seed that had planted itself in her mind and grown into nearly an obsession. Thinking about him made her heart race, and her breath come faster. This flourishing fantasy had to be killed before it drove itself between Gary and her.

Problem was, Molly didn't know how to kill it.

She was sleeping hard when she heard the screaming. Dug was at the back door barking before she could get dressed and oriented. An odd smell filled the air, like…burning.

Smoke.

She grabbed Dug's leash and lashed him to it quicker than she ever had and darted out the back. An eerie orange glow pierced the darkness to the west.

Holy shit. Molly's neighbors weren't up, and she didn't know what to do, so she and Dug ran for Burt's house. The street seemed to run parallel to the glow, and she kept her eyes on it the whole time.

Molly pounded his door, but no one answered. *Maybe he already knows?*

Then, she thought of Beth and her family, followed closely by Jimmy. Their homes were in opposite directions. Deciding Jimmy could probably fend for himself, she ran west towards the glow. It got brighter and smokier as she ran with the wind in her face. She choked on ash and panic when she realized the wind was blowing the fire towards the beach, and most of the town stood in its way.

The McMiller household was close enough to the blaze to hear the dull roar of flames. Molly pounded on their door relentlessly. Dug barked, adding to the noise. After her hands were raw, she finally heard movement inside.

Seth answered the door bare-chested and bleary-eyed. The sight of him took her breath away and she forgot why she was there.

"Molly?" He mashed his palm into his left eye.

"Seth. There's a fire." There. Message delivered.

"What?"

"FIRE!" She yelled and pulled him out onto the porch. She pointed towards the light in the uncomfortably close distance.

"Holy shit!" He yelled, voicing Molly's sentiments. He turned back into the house, "Beth, Mom! Get up! FIRE!" Then he ran straight for the blaze.

"Wait! What are you doing?"

"We have to do something!" he shouted back, not taking the time to look back at Molly as he ran.

She decided against arriving empty-handed and went into the house. She found Beth and her mother coming downstairs. "What's going on?" Beth asked.

"Beth! There's a huge fire! We have to get it out before it takes out the whole town."

"Oh my God. What can we do?"

Molly ran to the kitchen and collected as many deep pots as she could find. "Do you have any buckets or anything?"

"Yeah, I think so, in the garage."

"Grab them, and meet me at the well!"

By the time they arrived, a group was gathered at the well, including Burt.

"Hey." Molly said as they approached. Dug wagged his tail and Burt patted him on the head absently. "What's the plan?"

"Well, I think we're trying to come up with one."

"What about forming a chain and passing water down and trying to douse it that way?"

"I don't have any better ideas. I don't think it'll be effective enough, but we have to try something. Jimmy's down there with a bunch of guys throwing sand on it to try and keep it from spreading."

"Great! Keep them there, don't you think? Enough water might just tip the scale."

So that's what they did. People lined up in the

darkness and passed buckets of water one way, empty buckets the other.

Despite the cooler temperatures of the night air, they were all sweating from the work. Molly tied Dug to her ankle to free her hands and he sat patiently at her feet while they worked.

After what seemed like hours, word from what had been deemed the front line wasn't good. The fire wasn't spreading *per se*, but it wasn't going out, either. The woods where it was burning were dry from lack of rain, and the arid grass added fuel. It was burning dangerously close to a few homes, and no one was sure how long they could keep at it.

Beth stood next to Molly passing buckets. "Where do you think Seth went?"

"He's probably one of the ones throwing sand on the fire, don't you think? He ran straight for it."

She frowned. "I hope he's being careful."

Molly's arms burned with fatigue. She wasn't sure how much longer she could keep passing water. As the sun crested the horizon, a grey sky was revealed. "Maybe it'll rain and put the fire out," she hoped out loud.

"I think it's been cloudy for quite some time, Molly. I couldn't see the moon when we came down here."

Molly hadn't noticed. If that was true, these clouds weren't their savior.

Finally, Molly had to sit down. The sun had been up for a while, and if it could be seen, she estimated it would be clearing nearby roofs. Beth kept passing, and when Molly stood back up, she took a break. They traded back and forth like that until Mrs. McMiller came by with a loaf of bread and some water.

"Get some nourishment, girls," she insisted. Beth took hers first, then Molly. They couldn't totally stop the flow of water, or the fire would win.

"Have you seen Seth?" Molly asked.

"No." Gone were Mrs. McMiller's words of faith,

assurance and hope.

"I'm sure he's fine."

She only nodded and kept walking with her "nourishment."

Molly turned to Beth as she passed the bucket of water. "He's fine." *He has to be. He's just busy fighting the fire, like we are. Jimmy is there. He'll keep those guys safe,* she thought.

Then it happened. Molly felt a rain drop. She looked around, searching for others, but didn't see any. She thought she'd imagined it, but her shoulder was wet. "Beth," she started, and then a fat drop hit Beth square on the top of the head.

"Oh," she said.

Their saving grace rained down harder than they'd seen in weeks, and they all stood in it, laughing. Molly looked at Beth and they put their buckets down and started running. Molly forgot about Dug, though, and tripped over the leash tied to her ankle. She tumbled spectacularly to the ground.

Beth turned to see if she was OK. "No, no, I'm fine, go on! I'll be right behind you." Dug was confused, but excited to be running after sitting for so long, and they were up and on Beth's heels quickly.

When she arrived at the edge of the smoldering fire, Beth was looking north and south, rapidly scanning for her brother. The steam and smoke made it difficult to see clearly. Molly jogged along the burnt remains of the field, searching for Seth. People, mostly men, were lying on the wet grass, faces towards the heavens, utterly spent. None of them were Seth.

She did spot Jimmy sitting in the charred remains of a grassy area. He was filthy, soot on his face and covered in the dirt he'd been flinging on the fire. She smiled at him, relieved to see he was OK. He took a drink from a metal can and nodded her way.

She still hadn't seen Seth, so she doubled back and

spotted him. He was hugging Beth, his back to Molly. Their mom had caught up with them as well and was resting her hand on his shoulder, misty-eyed. Molly skidded to a halt at the scene. A complete family. She smiled. No one was hurt. They were all there, and she wasn't one of them.

She looked down at Dug. "Well, I guess we should go home."

She turned to walk away and heard her name.

"Molly!" Beth called out. She turned to see her break her embrace with Seth and run towards Molly. Seth quickly overtook her and gathered her in his arms, jerking Dug's leash.

"I'm so glad you're safe," he breathed into her hair.

"What else would I be?"

He put Molly down and she glanced uncomfortably at Beth. She cleared her throat. "You wanna come back to our place for a bit? Grab some lunch or dinner, or whatever it's time for?"

Molly looked to Mrs. McMiller for approval and she smiled. "I don't know. Maybe you guys should be alone, get some rest."

"Nonsense, dear. Come get a bite with us."

After they ate whatever meal it was supposed to be, their mom announced she was going to take a nap. Molly settled heavily into their couch and Seth sat down next to her, as close as he could get without touching her.

They were all exhausted, and their chatter petered out before long. Molly snuggled down into the couch a little further and was asleep before she knew it.

When she woke up, Dug's head was in her lap. She was confused for a moment, not remembering where she was. She blinked a few times, and then realized an unfamiliar weight was draped on her shoulders and her head was resting against something warm. She glanced down and saw Seth's bare stomach. She was leaning on him, practically cuddling with him.

Molly jerked away from him, roughly moving his arm in the process, and he woke up. "What time is it?" He didn't even acknowledge their positioning.

She looked out the nearest window. "It's dark again."

He stretched. "Mmm."

Beth was asleep in a nearby chair. "Want me to walk you home?" Seth asked.

She hesitated. *No, I don't.* She wanted to end this behavior that so frequently danced on the line between appropriate and not. But she also didn't want to walk home alone in the dark. Dug yawned lazily. "I have Dug with me. We should be fine."

"Wrong answer. Let's go."

She kept Dug between the two of them as they walked back to her house. They were both tired, so the walk was quiet at least. When they got to her doorstep, she turned to him. "Well, thanks for walking me home, Seth."

He looked deep into her eyes, admiring their beauty. Molly wondered if he enjoyed turning her insides to jelly that way. "Anytime."

"I'm glad you guys are safe, and your house is too."

"Me too. I mean, you too. I mean," he sputtered. "You know what I mean."

She chuckled inwardly. He was usually so smooth. Usually it was Molly doing the sputtering.

He closed the distance between them and raised his hand to her face. He hooked a stray hair behind her ear. "I mean, I don't know what I would do without you." He looked into her eyes and she could only gaze back.

Think about Gary. She cleared her throat. "Well, have a good night, Seth. See ya." Before he could make any more of the evening, she went inside and closed the door. She didn't even see Jimmy watching the scene unfold.

27.

In the morning Gary took the stairs two at a time as he raced to see Julia. He'd just finished pulling his white undershirt over his head when he came to a halt in front of her. She didn't seem startled in the least.

He was breathing hard from the effort, but he managed to get it out. "She's my wife."

"Well, there's some news if I ever did hear it."

"She's my *wife*, Julia," he said again, putting more emphasis on wife.

She stepped around Gary to retrieve the teakettle from the wood-burning stove. "I heard ya the first time, child. Do you know what her name is? Or where she's at? Whatcha gone do 'bout it?"

He sat heavily in the nearest chair. "I don't know. I don't know who she is, or how to find her. What can I do?" This time, he didn't want some pearls of wisdom from a quirky semi-old woman. He wanted a genuine answer. He waited anxiously for a response as she put two cups on the table and filled them with steaming water. She plopped the tea leaves in matter-of-factly, and sat herself in the chair with the same regard.

"Well. I 'spect you gonna hafta wait. Nothin' else for

ya."

Gary knew the conversation was closed. It wasn't the answer he wanted. He needed to do something. Act on this information. But there was so little to go on, what else *could* he do but wait? Wait, and hope she was waiting too.

28.

In the days following the fire, the damage was assessed and the cause of the fire was deemed natural. A handful of families had lost their homes, and it was discovered that two families were killed. A section of the wall was damaged where the fire came through, so the townspeople worked hard and managed to repair it in less than a week. The one good thing was that they hadn't lost any crops or the supply stores. So, once the displaced families moved in with other people in the neighborhood and the wall was repaired, normalcy – if you could call it that – returned.

On Saturday, an unexpected knock brought Molly out of her routine. Dug barked and she leaned the broom against the wall in the kitchen. "Just a sec!" she called.

She wiped her hands on the front of her shirt and walked to the door.

Jimmy loomed on the other side, and startled her a little. She laughed at herself. "Hey Jimmy. What a nice surprise. What's up?"

"I saw you with the McMiller boy."

She was confused. "Seth?"

"Is that his name? All I know is it sure as hell isn't Gary."

Molly shifted her weight in the doorway and looked up at Jimmy. "What exactly do you mean by that?"

"You know what I mean, Molly." He unfolded his arms and his tone softened a little. "Listen, these are hard times for all of us, but it's no time to be giving in to every little temptation that walks by."

She narrowed her eyes at Jimmy. "I appreciate the advice Jimmy, and I will certainly keep it in mind. However, there is nothing going on between Seth and I."

Jimmy scoffed. "Didn't look like nothin' from where I was standin'."

Molly threw her hands up. "Well I don't know where you were standing, Jimmy. Quite frankly, it's none of your business!" She regretted the barb immediately.

He frowned, and nodded. "You're right. I'll mind my business in the future."

"Wait, Jimmy, I'm sorry, please…" It all came out in one stream of words that bounced off of Jimmy's unyielding back.

By the time he reached the end of her driveway, tears brimmed in her eyes. *What is wrong with me? He's absolutely right, and I just jumped all over him.* She closed the door and resolved to stay focused on Gary, but doing that brought its own set of unanswered questions.

That afternoon, Molly went to Beth's. She felt lost. The chaos of the fire had put all of her issues on the back burner, but they all came screaming back with Jimmy's visit.

Why haven't I heard from Gary? Where is he? And how does Seth play into it? The questions repeated themselves over and over in her mind, plaguing her.

Beth answered the door, and before she could say hello, Molly blurted out, "Do you think he's fallen in love with someone else, and that's why he hasn't come home?"

Beth let out an incredulous breath and opened the door wider. "Won't you come in?"

Molly pushed past her, bringing a tornado of emotions into Beth's home. "I mean, what if he's met someone, fallen in love and sees no point in trying to get back here? He'd pretty much have to walk back if he was coming, anyway. Who'd go to all that effort if they had a perfectly good woman right where they were?"

"Hold on. Start over. What happened to the other options? He's on his way and just hasn't made it yet, or he's sitting tight wherever he is waiting for the power to come back on so he can come back here? What happened to those more rational approaches?"

"After the fire and everything else we've been through, I was just thinking, what if he met a woman? What would he do? Would he even want to come back here? Why would he?"

She interrupted Molly's stream of questions. "So…what prompted this sudden…revelation?"

That touched a nerve, and Beth could tell. "Nothing, it's just been so long since we've so much as spoken to each other. I'm worried, is all. Those girls at the airport were always flirting with him. It could be one of them. He could still be in Philly, getting her pregnant by now."

"No, really. What got your wheels turning in this direction?" Beth considered for a moment. "You were fairly fine when you left last night. Did something happen with Seth? Did he say something to you about men's needs," she put air quotes around 'men's needs', "or something like that?"

"No, Seth didn't say anything to me. It's not his fault. It's my own. I'm the one that planted the seed."

"What? What seed?"

"Hmm? Nothing."

Beth looked Molly square in the face. "OK, if you didn't come over here to have a rational conversation that I can participate in, why are you here?"

She sank down into the nearest chair feeling defeated. "I just needed someone to talk to, is all."

"Right, but what we're doing here isn't talking. It's going around in circles. You're avoiding whatever is really bothering you."

Molly looked at the pattern on the wall and didn't say anything.

Beth had one more thing in her bag of tricks. "Well, I was at a pretty interesting part in my book, so I'm going to go back to reading now if you're just going to stare at the wall."

Molly knew it was baloney. Beth hated to read. Nevertheless, she stood and made for the door.

Seeing the opportunity to clear the air go with her, Molly spoke up. "Fine." *What will she think of me? Now I've really done it. I finally have a confidant and just as quickly I throw her away.*

Beth sat down across from Molly and folded her hands in her lap, looking intently at her friend. When Molly didn't say anything, she prompted her. "Well, let's have it!"

"Fine."

"You said that already."

"Yes." Molly paused, trying to find the right words. Problem was, there were no right words. This wasn't supposed to be happening. Gary was supposed to be there. They were supposed to be together.

Beth saw the struggle playing out on her friend's face. "Maybe if you just-"

"I've developed a bit of a crush on Seth. And I thought if I had done that, maybe Gary had too, so why would he want to come home?"

"Um…What?" She burst out laughing. Molly frowned. "Wait a sec. Lemme get this straight. *You* have a *crush* on my *brother*?"

"I know. I'm terrible. I'm a horrible wife."

She'd stopped laughing, but was still smiling. "Now now, don't get carried away. It's been over three months without any contact from him. You're likely to get a bit lonely. You're only human. It's what you do with those feelings that determines what kind of wife you are."

Molly stared at the wall. The floral pattern made her wish for a simpler time. "One moment of weakness is all it would take. What if he acted on a moment of weakness? How would I feel?"

"How would you feel? That's good to keep in mind if you're ever…tempted." She smirked. Molly glared. "I'm sorry, but Seth? Really?"

"It doesn't matter *who* it is," she said, Jimmy's words echoing in her mind. "It just matters that it's not Gary."

Beth cleared her throat, trying to regain her composure. "So, what do you want me to say, then? How can I help you with this?"

"I don't know." Then a thought occurred to Molly. "What would you do?" she asked hopefully – not sure if she was hoping for permission or help staying away.

"Well, I'm not sure. On the one hand, Gary could very realistically be dead, and you could be keeping your life on hold for no reason."

Molly gasped at the thought.

"On the other hand, you could start a relationship with someone, and he could show up at your door at any minute. He could be there now wondering where you are. And based on your reaction to the thought of Gary being dead, I'd say you're not really ready to move on with that, are you?"

"No. I love him very much. This new thing is just…" Molly searched for the right word. "It's just an infatuation. Nothing more, nothing less. But the temptation is terrible because Seth is here now. I have the capability to meet my needs now. Today."

"Right, but those are all short-term needs. Think about what you want a year from now; ten years from now. The dreams you had for your life. Are you willing to throw those all away? It's one thing if you find out Gary did die that day, or someday between then and now, but it's quite something else to choose to throw all that you built together away simply because he's not here right now."

Molly felt stupid. *She's absolutely right. I'm acting like an impulsive idiot. I need to grow up and act like the married adult I am.* "Thank you, Beth. You're totally right."

She seemed surprised that Molly accepted what she had to say so quickly. "Oh, OK, great!"

They sat quietly for a few moments. "What now?"

"Got plans for the day?"

"Besides my excellent book? Nope!"

Molly smiled and shook her head, glancing at the beautiful day just beyond the window. "Let's go to the beach. I'll meet you over there in like a half hour. Sound good?"

"Sure!"

"Does what sound good?" Seth said as he came into the room.

"We were just talking about going to the beach."

"That sounds great, lemme change and I'll be ready!"

"Um…didn't you have to take care of Mrs. Bradleman's yard today?" Beth asked uneasily.

"Done and done. I have the whole rest of the day to myself, and now I get to share it with one pretty lady and one I tolerate."

Molly spoke up. "Well, if you're only going to tolerate me, then maybe you should stay home."

The game was on, and Molly was too caught up in it to care about who was breaking the rules.

The beach was on the other side of the wall, but not by much. They were in sight of the patrol, so they felt safe going for a little while, anyway.

It was seventy-five and sunny that January day. Molly wore a suit, but under shorts and t-shirt.

Especially with Seth on his way, what was I thinking? she wondered. He had an impeccable knack for making her forget who she was. She spread a blanket and plopped down. Just as she was unpacking her beach bag, Beth plopped down next to her. Molly made sure to sit on the very edge of the blanket, so Seth would have to sit on the other side. But he went ahead and spread a towel out next to her and sat down on that, leaving Molly in the middle of the two of them. She looked pleadingly at Beth, but her friend had no answers at the moment.

Beth was wearing a very cute purple sundress made of linen. It was sleeveless and flowy – perfect for the beach. Seth had donned board shorts and a white cotton button-down shirt, which he'd already unbuttoned, revealing a chiseled middle and beautifully sun-kissed skin. Molly started to sweat and her mouth went dry, but it wasn't because of the weather.

He stood abruptly, breaking her concentration. "Anyone for a swim?" His shirt melted off him and landed on the towel he'd laid out.

"No thanks. I'm not warm enough yet," Beth said.

"Molly? Come on! You're no wuss like Beth here," he goaded.

"Yes, actually I am a wuss like Beth. I think I'd like to just chill in the sun for a bit."

"Suit yourself. You girls can giggle about me behind my back. That's fine."

"Hey, you chose to spend the day with a couple of women. This is what you get." Molly said, not letting him play the feel-sorry-for-me-card.

He turned smug and dashed towards the shoreline.

"What the hell?" Molly said as soon as he was out of earshot.

"I know. I don't know what to tell you, except every other time I've seen him act like this around a girl, it's because he likes her. You better stay on top of it." She caught herself immediately. "NOT SETH! The problem! Keep it under control!"

Molly smiled as she got more flustered.

She sighed. "You know what I mean. I've seen him with girls he's interested in. Despite the fact that he's a total turd bucket to me, he can be pretty charming when he wants to be. He's pretty indiscriminate when it comes to whether a woman is taken or not. If he likes a girl, he goes after her, simple as that." She paused. "What I'm saying is, don't let your guard down if you care at all about Gary."

"Problem is, my guard tends to disintegrate around him. I don't even realize I've let it down until I'm alone, replaying the events."

"Yes, well, this I can see," she said as they watched Seth wade into the ocean, hooting and hollering about how it wasn't that cold, although they could both see him on his tip toes, trying to keep the important parts dry as long as possible.

"What am I gonna do?" Molly asked, a hint of desperation leaking into her voice.

"Not make a move on my brother."

"That's the easy part."

"And don't let him make a move on you."

Molly sighed. "That part will be a little more difficult."

29.

It was over a week before she visited again. Every night Gary went to bed hopeful, and in the morning he woke devastated that he had no more answers than before. Julia said to be patient, that these things couldn't be rushed. But Gary didn't feel he could afford patience.

She's waiting for me. He hoped.

He felt terrible having forgotten such an important aspect of his life. *What kind of husband was I to have completely forgotten a woman I may have spent years with?* he thought. Every moment the memories stayed out of reach was agonizing. He threw himself into work on the farm, trying to exhaust the guilt away. But even that didn't help.

When he finally saw her again, he dreamt he was in a nice restaurant. It had a modern feel to it, with dark tables, a waterfall with white flowers floating in the pool at the bottom as its centerpiece, and fresh red roses everywhere, decorating the tables. The plates were a slate color with red napkins to match the roses, and the finest crystal he'd ever seen for glassware. He nodded his head in approval as he appraised the place. Then, his eyes fell on her.

She approached from the opposite side of the room. She wore a sleeveless wrap-around dress, the color of the roses, which hugged her curves beautifully. The bottom of it flowed mysteriously around her as she walked, giving her a mystical air.

She approached the table and clasped her hands in front of her. "Hi," she said. Her voice was like music to his soul. It wasn't deep, but it was lower in tone than he had expected for her size. It also had a fair amount of confidence, making her even more attractive.

"Hi." Gary cleared his throat. "Welcome. Sit down!" He gestured towards the seat across from him.

"Thank you." She sat and paused for a moment, smiling casually. Gary could feel his hands becoming damp. "So, Gary, what do you do?"

Gary launched into the story of his budding career as a pilot, and she rewarded him frequently with a dazzling smile. She explained she was moving north in August to finish out her degree in English. They sat and chatted for hours, and the scene began to blur. Key words floated past his mind's eye, like *writer* and *college professor*.

He woke more slowly than he had from the first dream about her. He felt heavy, weighed down with information he didn't understand.

In the morning, Gary relayed everything to Julia. She sat quietly across from him, drinking her tea. After he finished telling her everything, he waited impatiently for her to give an assessment. When she didn't offer any words of wisdom, he prompted her.

"Well, what do you make of it?"

"I think the more important question is what do *you* make of it?"

"Maybe it was our first date. I wish she'd said her name. The entire night I didn't say it once. I wonder if she thought that was strange."

"Now, don't you go overanalyzin' it. This is just your version of what prolly happened. It's possible you've forgot or just plain left out some of the details. We know fo' sho' you left out a pretty important one – that child's name." Gary frowned. "Well, you think some more on it.

Everything'll come back in its own time. You'll see. Now, quit crowdin' my kitchen."

She shooed him out the door and he landed on the back porch, surveying the acres of work in front of him. He was torn between the happiness of seeing her again, and the frustration that he really didn't know any more than he did yesterday. He didn't know anything important, like what her name was, or where she lived. Those were the things he needed if he was ever going to find her.

He didn't even know how long ago the dream was. *Did I ever become a pilot? Is that what I did? Is that why we weren't together? Was I away from home during the Blackout?* He felt like screaming. Every time he got an answer, twenty more questions popped up.

Feeling defeated, he looked up at the sky. It was a deep purple with brilliant shades of red cresting over the horizon. *Please God, let me find her,* he prayed. *Please.*

30.

Molly was successful in avoiding Seth for most of the week. She and Beth stayed busy with school, and after school Molly kept to herself, so as not to attract unwanted attention. It worked until Saturday.

Molly was busying herself trying to dust and sweep and basically get the house fairly clean without any kind of assistance from an electric appliance – which was a frustrating task in and of itself – when someone knocked on the door. She leaned the broom against the door jam and went to see who it was. She hadn't spoken much to Jimmy since her outburst, so she knew it wouldn't be him. To her surprise and horror it was Seth, unaccompanied.

"Uh, hey Seth. What's up?"

"Hey stranger. Everything OK? I haven't seen much of you lately."

She shifted her weight from one leg to the other. "Yeah, we've been sort of busy this week."

"So I noticed. But, since it's Saturday, I thought you might want to hang out. No school today! No excuses!"

"Ya know, I'd love to Seth, but I'm kinda in the middle of something here."

He playfully brushed at the bandana containing her hair. "So I see. Come on, that can wait! It's beautiful out!"

She folded her arms and leaned against the doorframe. "What do you have in mind?"

"We could ride bikes, or go for a hike, or go to the beach again. Whatever you want."

"No, because what I want is to stay here and finish cleaning."

"OK fine. How about this? I help you finish up and then we enjoy this glorious day?"

He drove a hard bargain, but Molly wasn't wild about the idea of spending the day alone with Seth. It offered too much temptation.

She eyed him suspiciously. "What's Beth doing today?"

"Helping Mom go through some stuff, old clothes and stuff to give to the Center." The Center provided all kinds of things for anyone who needed them; canned goods, clothes, sheets, pots and pans. Although the store-bought canned goods were running low, a few of the residents who had Mason jars and knew how to can the old-fashioned way would leave extras for the Center. People were also going through their attics and coming up with all kinds of things to help each other out. Everyone had been down to the Center at least once for something. Molly went for some new towels when the salt water had finally destroyed hers. Since they put the well in, the towels were lasting much longer.

"I see." So, she was alone in fighting this.

"Hey, if you don't want help cleaning, I can go find some other woman to help with her weekend chores."

Molly sighed. She was too old for that kind of drama. So she let him turn and start to walk away. She smiled. *This is win-win for me. Either he'll keep walking and my problem would be solved, or he'll turn around and start begging.*

When he reached the bottom step of the porch, he chose option B.

"Come on, Molly. You don't really want to spend the whole day alone, do you?" It was bordering on whining.

"Wow. Sounds to me like *you* don't want to spend the day alone. If you're so eager to help someone, why don't you help your mom and Beth go through the stuff for the Center?"

"They're not as good company as you are." He looked Molly straight in the eye when he said it. He was laying it on thick.

She threw her hands up. "Fine. But you have to help me! You can't distract me, or keep me from finishing this!"

"Great!" He bounded up onto the porch, skipping all three steps. Dug greeted him happily once he was in the house, and Seth sat down on the floor to shower him with attention.

"Boy, that looks like help if I ever saw it."

He laughed. "Wow, you're quite the slave driver, Mrs. Bonham."

When he said her name that way it brought her back to reality. *Don't forget who you are,* she thought. *You are Mrs. Gary Bonham. Very much a devoted wife in a loving relationship. Any day now, he will be home and you can pick up where you left off.*

"And don't you forget it."

He laughed. "So, where do you want me to start?"

"I'm almost done down here." She handed him the broom. "Just finish sweeping, and meet me upstairs when you're done."

"Yes sir!" He saluted her in a ridiculous fashion and she couldn't help but laugh.

And so, that was how she spent the better part of her Saturday. Cleaning her house with a very attractive friend. Occasionally they bumped into each other, and shared a moment of eye contact. But, for the most part, they worked in quiet company. Molly decided it was nice to have help, and also not to be alone.

When they were done, they stood next to each other in the entryway, surveying their work. "A job well done if I do say so myself," Molly said.

He put his arm around her and she tensed a little. "We make a good team, you and I."

"Yup." She squirmed out of his grasp to go put the broom away, grateful it was still in her hands. When she closed the closet door, he was standing there watching with a half-smile on his face. He seemed content. She looked back and forth, unsure of what to do next. "OK, so now what?"

"I tell you what, get cleaned up and meet me out front of my place in half an hour."

"For what?"

"It's a surprise!" he said, already on his way out the door.

So she cleaned up and put on some jeans and a tank top. Nothing fancy. This was just some time with a friend. She didn't need to impress him.

She decided to take Dug along for whatever excursion Seth had in mind. He'd mentioned wanting to spend time outside, so she thought Dug could serve as a good distraction, and an excuse if she needed to extricate herself from an uncomfortable situation.

Seth was waiting at the end of his driveway when they walked up. He looked puzzled for a moment, but recovered quickly.

"Hi. I thought I'd bring Dug, since you seemed so gung-ho about doing something outside."

"Yeah, that's great." He had a canvas bag over his shoulder, and was dressed casually – dark blue jeans and a t-shirt. Nothing fancy. He pointed towards the direction he wanted to go and moved to put his arm around Molly, but she acted like she didn't notice, and maneuvered Dug between them.

She smiled internally. *Already having Dug is proving to be a good idea.*

Dug walked happily along, and Seth calculated his next move.

To break the tension, Molly asked, "So, you wanna tell

me where we're going now, or are you gonna make me wait until we get there for a dramatic reveal?"

He laughed. "Hmm…dramatic reveal sounds like fun. I opt for that."

So they walked along, settling into a comfortable silence. The birds sang beautifully as they took a turn onto a wooded path. The trees made a magical-looking canopy over their heads, and the sun dappled the ground.

"Huh," Molly said. "All the years I've lived here, and I didn't know this little trail was here." It was hard to believe this little gem was inside the wall, so close, just waiting to be discovered. Dug was having the time of his life, tail in the air and nose to the ground.

"Well, stick with me, kid, and you'll learn all kinds of things."

"Well thank you. That's rather haughty of you."

He laughed.

Then the woods opened up and the canopy became a prelude to something more beautiful than Molly could have imagined. There was soft grass stretched out before her, and to the left a beautiful blue pond that glittered in the sunlight. In the distance, a single tree with branches that extended farther than it seemed they should stood near the shoreline, providing the perfect amount of shade and beauty. They were the only ones in the clearing, with only the whisper of a breeze in the grass and the songs of the birds for company.

She was flabbergasted. "Wow, Seth, this place is really amazing. How did you find it?"

He shrugged. "Meh. I poked around a lot when I was a kid. Found quite a few spots like this. None were as nice as this one, but ya know. If you look around a little bit, this part of Florida is really quite nice."

He started walking and she stood there dumbly. "I always thought this part of Florida was nice," she said smugly.

She and Dug took their time getting to the tree,

needing to investigate every new smell, and by the time they arrived, Seth had a blanket spread, some crackers and a thermos set out, and was lounging against the trunk of the tree, staring out at the lake. He was quite a sight to behold as they approached.

"Why don't you let Dug explore a little bit?" Seth suggested as she sat down with Dug panting excitedly. As much as she was using him for a security dog, she knew he would love to sniff around freely. He was a good dog and wouldn't go far, and under normal circumstances she would have taken him off-leash ages ago. Thinking of how joyous he would be running in the grass made her forget about her own problems and she took the leash off, freeing her from the one tether to safety.

Dug trotted away happily and she frowned, watching him go. Seth laughed. "Jeeze, Molly, he's a good boy. He won't run off."

"Hmm? Oh, no, I know. I just…" She paused, scrambling for an explanation. "I don't know this area very well, so if he gets too far away I might not be able to find him."

He leaned back against the tree and folded his hands behind his head. "Well, then we'll just have to stay here until he finds his way back to us."

She stretched out on the blanket next to Seth while Dug sniffed around the shoreline. She closed her eyes, soaking it in. "Ya know, Seth, I quite enjoy your slice of paradise."

"Me too."

Molly dozed off. In her dream, she was in the field with Gary. She was lying with her head in his lap while he leaned against the tree. He was running his fingers lazily through her hair while Dug rested his head on her leg. They were complete. Everything was as it should be. She suddenly realized he was whispering. She scrunched her eyebrows, straining to hear him.

"*Wait for me.*" It was like a voice on the wind.

Haunting. *"Please God, let me find her."*

She woke with a start, and Seth lifted his hand. *Was he stroking my hair?* She looked at him, puzzled.

"You OK?"

"Bad dream."

"What was it about?"

"Nothing," she said shortly. She sat up and tried to straighten her hair, trying to decide if he'd been touching her or if it was just that the dream seemed so real.

"OK then. Want some crackers?"

"Sure," Molly said, grateful for something to keep her mouth busy.

They ate their snack and chatted lightly about nothing in particular as the sun started to turn the sky shades of pink – what his mom might find in the attic to take to the Center, what book she was reading, things like that.

He sighed heavily, clearly not wanting the day to end. By then, Dug was lazily stretched out on the blanket, just close enough for Molly to pet or give him a cracker.

"Well," Seth said reluctantly. "I s'pose we should head out before it gets too dark."

"Yes. I suppose we should."

They walked silently all the way back to Molly's house. She never bothered to put the leash back on Dug. He walked next to her, tired from the day.

When they got to the house, she opened the door for Dug and he trotted inside without so much as a goodbye to Seth.

He chuckled. "Well, I guess we tired the poor guy out."

"Yup. That was a great spot for him. Thanks for taking us there." She meant it, too. As risky as the day had been, she was glad she'd done it. They'd found a wonderful new spot, and spent a beautiful day outside. It was a good day.

"No problem." He smiled that gorgeous smile that melted her whole body. "Anytime."

She put her hand on the door, ready to follow Dug into the house. "OK, well, I'll see ya, Seth. Thanks again."

But when she turned to wave he was on top of her, closing in for a kiss. Each moment passed by like an eternity. She could see him coming closer, powerless to stop it, part of her wanting it, part of her horrified by it.

At the last moment, just as he was puckering up, she put her hands on his chest and pushed him away. "Seth, what are you doing?" It came out in her teacher voice, the one she use when she found one of the kids doing something bad.

"I'm sorry," He sputtered. "I just thought…since we'd had such a great day together…and you seemed like you really liked me…I guess I misunderstood."

She was sad in that moment. Sad to have to hurt him, and sad for the loss of what they might have shared. "Seth." She made sure to look him in the eye. "I'm married. I love Gary very much, and although he's not here right now, that doesn't erase my love for him. This will never happen between us." She didn't add *as long as Gary's alive* because she didn't want to leave an ounce of hope for Seth. She had to make sure this ended, here and now.

"OK," he said quietly. "I understand." As he turned and began to walk away, he said, almost to himself, "Gary is a lucky man."

Her heart broke. She went inside and shut the door. She sat down on the couch and cried. She cried for Gary. She cried for their future. She cried for Seth. But most of all, she cried for herself.

31.

Gary had been with Judd and his family for five weeks. To him, it seemed much longer than that, like an eternity, like he'd always been with them. He couldn't help but think it was five weeks of wasted time sitting, though, when he should have been trying to find her.

Little by little bits and pieces of information came back, but never all at once. One morning he remembered they had a dog. It was a shaggy-looking thing that Gary actually cared a lot about once he remembered him. But it took him another two days to remember the rest.

They'd gone to the shelter together that afternoon. They had been married for about two years, and she'd bugged him for a dog for at least that long. He agreed to go to the shelter just to look, so he told her to get any ideas of coming home with someone out of her head. She did surprisingly well. He could tell she left all her emotions in the car and walked into the shelter purposefully.

They separated for a bit. She was looking at puppies, but Gary found this one he couldn't seem to walk away from. He was smaller than the other two dogs in the pen with him, and getting trampled by them.

When she walked up, Gary said, "What do you think of this guy?"

"Which one? They are kind of all over each other."

"The little one." He was lighter in color and shaggy. Looked a little bit like the dog from Benji. Most of all, he just looked happy. Despite being caged outside during the Florida summer with an empty water bowl and two cellmates that were a bit overbearing, he seemed glad to be there. Like he thought he was right where he was supposed to be.

She found his paperwork attached to the door. "Says he's a two-year-old terrier mix, whatever that means. But that's as big as he'd get, which is nice." She looked him over. "He's a good size, I think."

"I like him."

"Well, do you want to see if they can take him out?"

"Yes. Yes, I do."

They took down his number and went to the desk. A few minutes later they brought him into a room where he could roam around. He was scared and wouldn't come close, but he wasn't opposed to being petted either. He was so thin.

"What do you know about him?" Gary asked the worker who brought him in.

"He's got a great personality, that's for sure. But he's been here thirteen days. Tomorrow is his last day with us."

"Oh, did you find someone to take him?" she asked. Gary couldn't tell if there was hope or disappointment in her voice.

"No, they have a two-week limit here. After that, they meet their maker."

"What?" she exclaimed.

"We'll take him," Gary said.

"What?" she said again.

"I'll leave you two alone." The worker left to wait just outside the door.

"We can't leave him here," Gary told her.

"I know, but I wanted a girl, and a puppy to boot." She looked at him. "He is very cute." She considered.

"OK. Let's get him!"

So they walked out with a dog because Gary couldn't walk away. It wasn't what he'd expected, that's for sure. But he considered it one of the best decisions they ever made.

Then, out of the blue, Gary had it. He knew what he needed to know. He was working in the orchard with Judd, trying to pick apples before the next frost, when it all came screaming back. Her name, what she did, what he did, where they lived, everything.

He dropped the basket of apples and they tipped over as he ran to Judd.

"Molly! Her name is Molly!" he yelled. Judd was startled, but Gary didn't care. "She lives in Florida, we live in Florida. She's a professor of English at a school near our house. She rides a scooter to work every day. We've been married over five years," he kept talking as Judd stared incredulously. "Judd, I'm a pilot! I work for a small corporate company. I was in Pennsylvania when the Blackout happened! That's why I'm alone! I walked here! Can you believe it?"

The memories kept coming back and suddenly he knew exactly who he was and where he was supposed to be, and Virginia wasn't it. "Judd, I have to go. I can't stay here any longer. I have to be with her."

"I'll walk with you up to the house. Let's try to make a plan, OK? If you're too hasty about it you might end up further behind. Ya know?"

"I guess. All I know is I've wasted a lot of time I should've been spending working my way south."

Judd was visibly hurt, and Gary regretted saying it immediately. "Well, I don't know about all that. You've been a big help around here. I know I'll sure miss ya," he said.

"Oh, jeeze, Judd, I didn't mean it like that. Of course I'll miss you, and I'll never be able to repay everything you and your family have done for me." He stopped walking and rested his hand on Judd's shoulder. "You saved my life, J."

He scoffed. "Well, I wasn't just gonna let ya lay there."

"All the same, thanks."

He cleared his throat. "Let's head on up t' the house and see if Momma and Pop got any ideas."

Julia was sewing at the kitchen table, patching some holes in Judd's coat for the winter, and his dad was out back. Judd went to get him while Gary sat with Julia.

"What's this about? You boys are supposed to be getting' them apples off'n the trees before we lose 'em."

"Julia. I've remembered."

"Remembered what?" she asked as she worked the patch on Judd's jacket.

"Everything."

She put down her work and looked at Gary. "Well, that's wonderful!" She paused, realizing what it meant. "I 'spect you'll be wantin' to head out then?"

"Yes ma'am."

"Well, don't you worry. We'll get you all sorted out before we set you loose."

He smiled, not really knowing what she meant by that. By then, Judd and his dad were walking up.

"What's this I hear 'bout you leavin', boy? What makes you think you worked off your debt so soon?"

"Henry!" Julia hollered at him. "Don't you listen to that old grouch. We gon' help any way we can."

Judd's dad smiled mischievously. "Well, ya cain't let him think he's gettin' off scott-free there, Julie baby. Gotta hassle 'im some."

Gary laughed, and they spent the rest of the day sitting at the table, planning his route, what supplies he should have, how long they thought it would take, and even when and where they thought he would need to stop.

It was decided that Gary would leave in the morning,

to get one more good night's sleep at their house, and so they could have a celebratory farewell dinner. As much as he needed to leave, he knew he had to stay for that. They'd become his family and he might never see them again.

So they spent the evening eating, laughing and just being together. Sitting there, looking at them laughing and talking easily, he realized what a blessing they'd been. It was then that Henry made an announcement.

He stood, banging his fork on his cup. "I'd like to make a toast." They all raised their glasses. "Gary, you've been a blessing to us, a real miracle in our own home. I just wanna say, we've been glad t'have ya. That's why we want to give ya' ole Thunder. He'll help ya get home a little faster."

Thunder was their best horse. "I don't know what to say. I can't possibly accept such a tremendous gift after everything you've done for me."

Julia spoke up. "You can and you will, boy."

Gary frowned. He wasn't going to win this one.

"Now, you take good care'a that horse ya hear? He's our best stallion, and I don't want no news he got stolen and butchered by them Wanderers. You protect him same way he'll protect you, got it?" Henry said.

"I will. I promise." Gary smiled.

"What you smilin' bout? You look like a kid on Christmas mornin'," Julia said.

"I was just picturing Molly's expression when I come riding up on Thunder. She won't know what to think of me."

"No, I 'spect she won't. 'Cept all I think she'll be carin' 'bout is that her husband come home. She prolly won't even see ole Thunder."

He smiled wider. *I am heading home.*

The Rainbow
32.

"God puts rainbows in the clouds so that each of us – in the dreariest and most dreaded moments – can see a possibility of hope."
– Maya Angelou

After a storm, the air clears and a whisper of hope sings anew. The windblown and desperate cling to the song, praying for it to carry them through the storm's wreckage to better times.

33.

After the so-called "come to Jesus" talk with Seth, things were a lot easier. He kept his distance for the most part, and Molly focused on school, the house, Beth, and what her plans were when Gary came home. It had been 101 days. She and Beth sat down and figured out how long it would take Gary to walk from Philly back home, and they estimated at least three months, if he didn't have any problems. Molly didn't want to think about what might happen if he didn't show up. She tried to remind herself that he could've gotten hung up somewhere, so she shouldn't be discouraged that he hadn't shown up right on day ninety.

That afternoon she was curled up on the couch, lost in *To Kill a Mockingbird*, when someone knocked on the door. Dug barked to alert her, on the off chance she hadn't heard the knocking. She marked her place and unfolded herself from the couch. "Yeah, just a sec!"

A breathless Beth stood at her door. "What's up?"

"A Wanderer," she puffed. "They caught a Wanderer." She put a hand on the doorframe to steady herself.

"What?" Molly processed the information. "Gary," she said and pushed past Beth, running for Burt's home.

Molly assumed Burt's house was where they would take a Wanderer, and Beth didn't have any better ideas as she struggled to keep up.

She burst through Burt's front door without even knocking. "Burt!" She called. "Is it Gary? Burt!" She heard some muffled sounds coming from the basement, so she darted down there.

Molly tripped over what she thought was a heap of clothes at the bottom of the stairs. She sat up and checked herself for injury, miffed about the obstruction. Beth caught up and helped her to her feet.

"Molly! What are you doing here?" One of the Watchers asked.

"James. What the hell?" She gestured toward the pile of clothes with a slightly battered hand.

"We found her outside the wall." A voice startled her from the darkness in the corner of the basement. It was Jimmy. "She proved to be uncooperative." He said as he moved into the light.

"Uncooperative with what, Jimmy? What the hell were you trying to get her to do?" Molly couldn't get her mind around a scenario where this outcome would be acceptable.

"That's not really any of your concern." He folded his arms across his chest and looked at Molly. The other men backed up, but Molly knew him too well to be intimidated.

"Don't give me that bullshit, Jimmy. Does Burt know about this? Does he know you're beating young women to a pulp for some mysterious purpose?"

"Burt knows what he needs to know."

"So no, in other words."

Jimmy frowned. Molly bent down to check on the girl. She was alive, but her breath gurgled, and there was fresh and dried blood covering all of her exposed skin. Beth cradled the girl's head in her lap while Molly tore some of the cloth away and dampened it with some spit to wipe at the girl's face. Jimmy simply stood by and watched.

When some of her fair skin was revealed, but already turning a nasty purple color, Molly looked up at Jimmy. "Well, now we're even, Jimmy."

He puzzled at her.

"I disappointed you, and you sure as hell disappointed me."

Once the girl was settled into the hospital, Molly headed back home. She was exhausted from the day, disgusted with what had happened, disappointed that it hadn't been Gary, and just ready to be done.

The hospital was really just someone's home that had the bottom floor stocked with supplies and beds. So, when Molly stepped out onto the front porch, she didn't even notice Jimmy.

"Molly, wait." He startled her, and she nearly fell down the steps to the sidewalk.

"Jesus, Jimmy. You scared me."

"Sorry." He paused. "For everything."

She narrowed her eyes at him. "Are you sorry because I can't understand why you did what you did, or sorry you carried it that far, or sorry it happened at all?"

He shifted his weight. "Everything, I guess."

She scoffed and shook her head.

"Look, it's so easy for you to pass judgment. You don't understand what we do to keep you safe, the sacrifices that must be made for the greater good."

"Sacrifices, huh? She's someone's daughter. Someone's sister, Jimmy. How would you feel if it was me someone had beat up like that?"

"You know what?" His voice rose with his anger.

"What?" she fired back.

He took a deep breath and lowered his voice. "I just wanted to say that I'm sorry, and was stupidly hoping you'd be able to see my side. Maybe not see me as such a monster."

He turned to walk away. She let him get to the end of the sidewalk before she said, "I could say the same thing to you."

He stopped dead in his tracks and reeled on her from on top of his soapbox. "What you were doing with Seth was just wrong, Molly." He jabbed his finger at her. "Gary is out there somewhere, trying desperately to get back home, and you thank him by cheating on him? What kind of wife does that?"

"Not this kind. You're the one who leapt to conclusions. I never cheated on Gary, with Seth or anyone."

Jimmy's finger froze mid-air, then fell limply by his side. He was defeated. "Sure, I thought about it. And yes, I was attracted to Seth, but I never acted on it. In fact, I told Seth he probably should stay away from me from now on. So you could say that I'm the kind of wife who's loyal, loving and devoted to her husband, even though we haven't seen each other or spoken to each other in," her voice broke as she started to cry. "In months. I know how easy it is to be on that soapbox, Jimmy. But for the rest of us, down here on level ground, we sure could use," she sniffled, "some understanding is all."

He closed the distance between them and embraced her. "I'm sorry. I'm sorry Gary isn't here. I'm sorry all this is happening."

She cried into his shoulder, saturating his shirt. It felt good to have her rock back, even if it wasn't Gary. "I'm sorry for what you had to do today."

He smoothed her hair. "Me too."

After a lot of rest and some coaxing, they learned the girl's name was Charlotte. She was a nursing student at a school in northern Georgia when the Blackout happened. Far from home, and worried about her family, she decided to make her way back. But, she hadn't calculated correctly, and the journey took far longer than she'd thought, so she ran out of supplies.

"Didn't you run into other Wanderers?"

"Yes," she said in a soft voice. "But most of them didn't bother me. I guess I wasn't enough of a threat? A few groups asked me to join them when they found out I was a nursing student, but I told them no, that I wanted to go home." She paused. "One group didn't take too kindly to that."

Molly frowned but didn't press her for details. "So, where is home, Charlotte?"

"Sanford."

"That's still, what do you think, Burt? A hundred miles from here?"

He nodded. "Yeah, thereabouts."

"So, what's your plan then, Charlotte?" Charlotte snuggled deeper into the blankets on her bed in response. "Mkay, well I see this playing out one of two ways. We'll give you what we can spare to help you get the rest of the way home, or you can stay here until the power comes back on." Burt cleared his throat. Clearly he didn't like the second idea. Molly ignored him. "But, if you decide to stay, you have to work. Everyone contributes to this community to keep it running. Since you were studying to be a nurse, I think this would be the best place for you." Charlotte looked around.

Burt frowned. "Can I speak with you a moment?"

Molly smiled down at Charlotte. "I'll be right back."

They went out onto the front porch for some privacy. "Molly, what are you thinking? She can't stay here with us! She's a Wanderer!"

"Burt, for Christ's sake, she's a person. You're as bad as Jimmy! She's someone's daughter! How would you feel if your daughter was separated from you and received such a reception as we've given Charlotte? Wouldn't you want to know someone was willing to help her?"

He didn't like the comparison one bit and it showed. "Molly. Please try to be realistic about this. Not everyone is as open-minded as you." He gestured towards the house where Charlotte lay. "These people have threatened us, killed us, taken our food, and destroyed our supplies. Jimmy is rightfully cautious." He looked Molly right in the eyes. "You can't expect her to have a happy, safe life with us."

Her gaze didn't waiver. "Don't you think that's sad?"

"Maybe it is. Doesn't make it any less true."

"Well, maybe we won't have to deal with it. Maybe she won't even want to stay here."

He shook his head. "And if she doesn't? Who will happily give up a portion of their rations to a Wanderer?"

Molly glared at him. "I will."

Charlotte decided not to stay, much to Burt's relief. Once she was feeling better, Molly loaded an old backpack with what she hoped would be enough food for ten days. She didn't give her enough water to last that long, because water is heavy to carry. Molly gave her two canteens full and told her to make finding drinkable water a priority along the way. She also gave her a bike. She decided it would help her cover the distance faster, and would serve her better than if Molly kept it.

Molly walked Charlotte to the wall, pushing the bike and going over the route with her again. "Just stick to I-95 south, and you'll be fine. Try to stay away from other Wanderers, now that you have things they might want, OK? Don't sleep on the road or in plain sight." Words tumbled out. "With the bike, it shouldn't take you more than a week to get home."

When they got to the gate, she turned. She seemed so young to be doing this on her own. But no one in the town wanted to risk their necks seeing her home safe. Molly would have gone, but she needed to be there if Gary came home. She said a silent prayer for the young girl's safety.

"I'll be OK, Molly. Thank you for everything." Molly

hugged her and she took the bike.

"Good luck. It was wonderful to meet you." She smiled at Molly and rode away. It was the last time Molly saw her. She could only hope that if Gary needed help out there somewhere, someone would be willing.

Saturday morning, after Charlotte left, Molly lay in bed, imagining Gary's return. She expected him to come through the door any day now.

A thought occurred to her, and she sat up in bed. *My door is protected by the wall. He'll have to get past the wall to come home. What if the Watchers don't recognize him and turn him away?* Panic set in. *Or worse? What if they treat him the way they treated Charlotte?*

She jumped out of bed, jostling Dug. She had to do something, but what? She stood in the center of the bedroom, thinking, when her eyes fell on Gary's face. Most of their pictures had been digital, trapped inside boxes with nothing but a black screen. A precious few were printed, framed and scattered throughout the house. The one on the dresser was a picture of the two of them on their trip to Greece last year. She grabbed it and ran her finger along Gary's face. They had such a wonderful trip. It seemed so long ago.

If I showed the picture to The Watchers, would they know him then? How would I possibly catch them all? Then, another thought hit her. *Am I the only one in town with a loved one on the other side?*

Picture in hand, she ran to Jimmy's house. She knocked on his door, hoping she didn't smell too much like sweat and outdoors.

Jimmy answered in shorts and a white undershirt, a towel slung over his left shoulder. "Hey Molly, what's up?"

"Jimmy, I was thinking, when Gary comes home, how will anyone know who he is? What if you or the other

Watchers mistake him for a Wanderer and won't let him in, or worse?"

He knew she was referring to Charlotte. "Well, that is something to consider."

"Is there anyone else in town with a similar situation? Relatives outside the wall?"

"I'm sure there are. I don't think anyone else has a spouse on the other side, but I know there are siblings or close friends out there. Everyone is worried for someone. What are you driving at, Molly?" he urged her to get to the point.

"What if we put up a bulletin board for the Watchers? That way, if they do come across a Wanderer, they can see if they belong here."

He was skeptical. "You know what happened with Charlotte was an isolated incident right? Seeing lone Wanderers is highly unlikely."

Molly didn't miss the implication that the incident was isolated because of Charlotte, not because the Watchers' reaction would be different next time. She decided to let it pass, for now. "No, I know, but I'd hate for someone's loved one to get turned away or..." She paused, "well, beaten because no one recognized them."

"But don't you think Gary would tell the Watchers he was your husband?"

"Do you think the Watchers would listen? Would you listen? After everything the Wanderers have done? After what happened to Charlotte?"

He sighed. "OK, Molly. Snag a bulletin board and post your picture. I'll make sure the Watchers study it. Heck Molly, I know it's been a while since I saw him, but I might even recognize him."

Molly hugged Jimmy around the neck. "Thank you! Gary will find his way home safely, I just know it!"

Jimmy chuckled sadly as he embraced her. "I'm sure he will, Molly."

THE BLACKOUT

The following Saturday, Molly got a few of the boys from class to drag a double-sided cork bulletin board down to Burt's basement. It was decided that if any more Wanderers were found or apprehended, that was where they would be held. She thought it best to have the bulletin board there for easy comparison.

After she thanked the boys and they left, she was alone with the empty board in Burt's basement. She looked at one of her only pictures of Gary and smiled, remembering when their lives weren't so broken. She hesitated to put the snapshot on the corkboard. It would mean leaving it there. One of her most valuable possessions was going to be exiled to someone else's basement indefinitely.

I should've thought this through. A tear ran down her cheek, washing away what had been and clearing the way for what was. She steeled herself and carefully pinned the image to the board, taking care not to poke a hole in that frozen moment in time.

Molly took a step back to look at her one lifeline to her husband. She sighed heavily. "OK, Gary," she said aloud to the dim room. "I hope this helps."

After one hundred and five days, Molly found herself needing to feel connected to Gary even more than usual. She wasn't sure if it was the constant expectation that he would walk through the door, or simply loneliness, but she needed to talk to him. So she dug out an old notebook and started to write to him. It helped tremendously, and she had no idea why she hadn't done it sooner. That night, she sat down at her desk with her brightest candle by her side and started to write to him.

Hi Gary!
Well, it's been 105 days since the Blackout. That's a long time to be without you, and wonder where you are and if you're OK. If you took a direct route, you should be home by now. If you went

along the coast it'll be a few more days I think. I can't wait to hear about what has happened to you, why it's taken you so long to get home, and what you had to go through to get here. It's been a mild winter here, and I hope you're far enough south by now that you can stay warm. Winter in the north without heat or a warm coat would be miserable.

I posted your picture on the board for all the Watchers to see, so hopefully you won't have any trouble from them getting home. You should've seen what they did to Charlotte. I'll tell you more about her when you get here.

Today was a school day. We're still reading Native Son with the older kids, and The Giver with the younger ones. They seem to be enjoying it. They're both interesting because they discuss issues of prejudice during a time when they had more than we do now. The kids can't really imagine judging someone as useless or less than someone else based on their age or skin color. One of them even said Mrs. Carroll (I don't know if you remember her or not) is great at making food and clothes, and even though she's old, a lot of people would be hungry and naked without her. I thought that was excellent.

You know, I didn't think I'd like teaching the younger kids. They're such a handful, not nearly as independent as my college kids. But it's so satisfying to see them really get something. To see their minds open to a whole new world of possibilities is very exciting for me.

Dug and I went for a nice long walk this afternoon. I think this weekend I'll take him to a new spot we discovered, with a lake and a tree and tons of grass to run around in, that's if the weather is nice.

I suppose that's about all I have to say for tonight. I hope you are doing well with your journey home, and know that I am waiting anxiously for you to get here! I love you so much and miss you more than words could say.

Love,
Molly

She sighed as she closed the notebook and carried the

candle to the nightstand. She changed clothes and got into bed, thinking about Gary.

Should I tell him about Seth? She felt a little guilty leaving news of Seth out. She didn't want to taint their reunion with news that another man had come on to her, and she had been tempted to act on it. But then again, she didn't want to wait too long, and have it turn into a giant secret.

Great, she thought. *Something else to obsess about and keep me awake tonight.*

The next day, after they sent the kids home, she asked Beth for her opinion. "Ya know, that's a sticky issue. It's not something I would purposely hide from him, but I'm not sure I'd come right out and tell him either. It might upset him. Assuming he comes home in the next few days, he's probably worked fairly hard to get here. If I were him, I'd be peeved if I'd nearly died trying to get back to you and you were off being tempted by another man. Even though you did the right thing, he may not be able to see that right away."

"I agree. I just don't want to be distracted by guilt if I finally get to see him again. I don't want that initial meeting to be cluttered by anything other than my joy at seeing my husband again."

"So don't let it. You didn't do anything wrong. You stayed faithful to your marriage, not even knowing if there was a marriage to be faithful to. I'd say that's pretty darn honorable if you ask me."

"Yes. You're right."

Molly paused, debating whether to ask the next question. She decided to dive in. "So, how's Seth?"

She smiled and shook her head. "He's a typical man." Molly looked questioningly at Beth. "Well, he's not wallowing in misery like I would be if someone had said the things you said to *me*."

Molly frowned and nodded her head. Oddly, she was stung by how little she had meant to Seth. But she didn't really want him pining over her, either.

"Isn't that what you wanted to know, Molly? That he wasn't devastated?"

"Well, yeah. A short period of mourning would have been nice, but whatever."

She laughed. "You are too much."

Molly shook her head rapidly, trying to get these ridiculous thoughts out. *Yes I am.*

They spent the rest of the afternoon chatting and planning the following day's activities.

That evening, Seth came around for the first time since their talk, to walk Beth home. Molly smiled and gave him a short nod. He nodded back at her and turned to Beth.

"You ready to go? Mom sent me down here to get ya because it was getting dark."

"Sure. Sorry." Beth gathered up her papers hastily, thinking they were uncomfortable. But they weren't. Molly was focusing on Gary, and Seth had moved on to his next potential conquest. She was back to being his sister's dorky friend, and she was fine with that.

That night, she didn't have a whole lot to say to Gary. She told him about the day's lessons and asked how his travels had been.

When she went to bed she kept thinking, *One hundred and five days. In a week, could I be lying here next to Gary? What on earth would I do with myself?*

She fell asleep with a smile on her face that night, thinking about lying next to Gary once again. She didn't even notice the slight hum her home was emitting as she drifted off.

34.

Thunderbolt doubled Gary's progress, but it would still take over a month to cross the distance between Virginia and Florida. Judd cautioned against pushing Thunderbolt too hard and killing him before they got home. So he tried to stay satisfied with doubling the pace, and, if Thunderbolt was in good spirits, going an extra few miles at the end of the day.

They stayed off the main roads to avoid other travelers. Judd's family had stocked them well with food and supplies, and Gary didn't want to lose any of that, including a well-fed horse.

At night, they found a spot deep in the woods and settled down. Thunderbolt understood the importance of quiet, and didn't make a sound.

Five days into their journey, they were just south of Plymouth, North Carolina when they heard rustling. Thunderbolt's ears pricked and Gary pulled on the reins, bringing the horse to a stop. They sat silently as the voices approached from the south. They were coming right at them.

He hopped off Thunderbolt and urged the beast deeper into the woods, in a direction Gary hoped wouldn't take them too far off course, but would keep them out of the path of the Wanderers.

He and Thunderbolt concealed themselves as best they could, and the Wanderers passed right by. It was a group of four, two women and two men.

"Earl, I'm exhausted. When can we stop and rest?"

Oh please, not here. Gary thought. Who knew how long they could stay there undiscovered if Wanderers made camp right smack in front of them.

"We cain't stop here. Quit your whinin'. We're close to Plymouth. Maybe we'll find somethin' there." Earl said.

The other woman piped up. "You said that about Greenville, New Bern and Willmington. What makes Plymouth so special?"

The man whirled around and slapped her. "You got any bright ideas, besides mouthin' off?" She brought her hand to her face and stayed silent. "You's welcome to go out on your own if you think you can do so much better. Ain't nothin' stoppin' you. Lord knows I won't. One less mouth to feed if you ask me."

She was more hurt by his comment than his slap. "No, of course you know best. I didn't mean anything by it. I'm just tired is all."

His whole demeanor changed then and he caressed her face where he'd smacked her and she flinched. "I know, baby. We'll be safe soon. Earl's takin' care a you." He paused, and a little menace found its way back into his voice. "Don't forget it."

They tromped on through the woods, never knowing they were being watched, or that they were less than a hundred feet from their temporary salvation.

Gary couldn't wait to be back home. It was exhausting being on guard constantly. He knew their home would be safe from threats like that, although he had no concrete information to base that assumption on. For all he knew, their little town could closely resemble Williamsburg. The thought made him want to vomit.

Gary sighed, pushing the image from his mind. Molly

would be there waiting for him. He knew it. She had to be. *If she isn't, I'm totally lost.*

That night, they stopped near a small town. They were far enough from it that no one would notice them, but close enough to keep an eye on comings and goings. It got dark early that time of year, but they just adjusted their schedule so they got up and moving earlier.

He snuggled down next to the tree Thunderbolt was tied to and dozed off.

Gary woke up with a start. He had no idea how much time had passed; it was still dark out, save for a glowing in the distance.

He squinted at it. It was coming from the town. *What is that?* he thought. He didn't hear anything. *Could it be a fire?* He didn't see any smoke rising. It was so dark, though, he wasn't sure he'd be able to see smoke at that hour.

Gary gathered his things and untied Thunderbolt, leading him on foot quietly closer to the light. He was mesmerized by it. *What could it be?*

As they got closer he could hear a low hum. A sound unfamiliar, but not totally foreign.

Suddenly, it hit him. "The power."

The Light
35.

"So the darkness shall be the light, and the stillness the dancing."
— T.S. Eliot

The light shone so brightly it blinded many. Chaos struggled to again take over. But for those who had learned the hard lessons of the past months, the light shined like a blessing and a curse. A reminder of the life they'd once had, and a choice to go back to it, or not.

36.

Molly woke up to Dug barking. He was standing in the doorway of the bedroom, just barking away. She started to holler at him, but then she heard knocking at the front door.

"Molly! You in there? Wake up!"

It was the neighbor next door. *What could he possibly need right now?* she wondered.

She stumbled to her feet and called out, "Yeah, just a sec." Dug barked a few more times and she shushed him.

"Enough, Dug. I'm up. It's fine."

Molly got to the door feeling disheveled but awake. "Hey, Chris. What's up?"

"What's up?!" He nearly yelled. It was too early, or maybe too late, for this.

"Yes, what is wrong? How can I help you?" *How can I get you off my front porch?*

"The power's on." He just threw it out there, like 'hey, did you see it's raining' or 'I had soup for lunch.'

He smiled and walked away, going to the neighbor on the other side. Was this some sort of ridiculous telephone game? 'Here's a big lie in the middle of the night, pass it down,' kind of thing?

Molly closed the door and locked it firmly behind her. Clearly Chris had been drinking.

That's when she noticed it - a red light brazenly shining at her from the ceiling. It was attached to the smoke alarm. She ran to it and stared. *Could it be?*

She darted to a nearby light switch. Dug followed her jerky movements exactly, wagging his tail like a windmill. She hesitated. This could be the moment. She reached up and flipped the switch. Nothing happened. She looked all around the room, becoming frantic. Why had nothing happened? The little red light glowed defiantly.

She smiled and exhaled the breath she didn't know she had been holding. That was an outlet switch. She moved to the one next to it and pressed it daringly. The whole room was bathed in light in the middle of the night. She collapsed to the floor and cried. Their prayers were answered. Power was restored. The Blackout was over.

So, where is Gary? she wondered, while she sat in the beautifully unnatural light.

37.

Gary sat with Thunderbolt in the woods, trying to decide what to do. It defied all logic to assume things would be normal, and he could waltz in there and expect to get some form of speedy transportation home.

More likely I'd be robbed, my horse stolen or slaughtered, or both, and left with nothing but the skin on my back, if I was lucky, he thought.

However, he found the temptation was hard to ignore. Before the Blackout, it would have been so easy to get home. Not a one-hundred-plus-day struggle, which still left him hundreds of miles from his goal.

What if I could just take a car and drive the rest of the way? I'd be home tonight. The thought was almost enough to make him step out onto the road. But he thought of Thunderbolt. What would Gary do with him if he was lucky enough to find a working car with enough gas to get them there? It wasn't like the horse would fit in the back seat.

Gary sighed heavily, resolved to continue on the current path. He wondered how much harder it would be now to remain concealed. People might be more active after dark with the return of the power. But with more activity came more noise. That he was OK with.

He thought about Molly as he walked Thunderbolt back to their camp. *Is the power on where she is? Had it ever gone out? Will she wonder where I am if I don't show up in the next few days? Will she think I'm dead, or not coming home? Did she decide I was dead weeks ago?* He tried to push the thoughts out of his mind. It wasn't that much longer, right? In the scheme of the journey, another twenty days wasn't such a big deal, was it? Maybe if he pushed Thunderbolt a little more they could make it eighteen or nineteen. He always told Molly, "I'd rather get home alive and late than on time in a box." She'd never really cared much for that sentiment. Gary didn't think it comforted her much on those nights she expected him home but got a call he'd be gone one more night.

He thought for a second. *At this point, I wouldn't make it home in a box. If something happened to me, Molly would never know. She would just wait and wait, until she could only assume I was dead, or wasn't coming home.* The thought hit him like a ton of bricks. *I can't let that happen to her. I won't let that happen to her.*

No matter what, he vowed he would be home in twenty days or less. *Twenty more days, Molly. Just hang on a little longer.* He said it as much to himself as he did to her.

38.

In the first few days after the Restoration, a recording broadcasted on the radio on a loop feed. Jimmy ran to Molly's house with his radio so she could hear it, and they later called a town meeting so everyone could hear.

It was a man's voice reading a letter from the government, though who the man was remained unclear.

My fellow Americans,

We are pleased to announce the recovery process has begun. Power has been restored in various amounts to most of the country at this point. However, please exercise caution. Brownouts and even blackouts are still frequent due to overloading the fragile system that's in place. We request you only utilize necessary systems for the time being.

It has become clear, and most scientists and government officials agree, that a catastrophic solar flare is what caused the Blackout. It's our understanding that the damage affected all of the north-western hemisphere. It is only through the aid of our allies in Europe that we were able to recover as quickly as we did.

As far as loss of life is concerned, officials hesitate to even provide an estimate at the current time. We do know the toll is far-reaching, and has affected a large number of you listening now, and for that, we express our deepest sympathies.

This is a time of hope. Abraham Lincoln once said, "My

dream is a place and a time where America will once again be seen as the last best hope of the Earth." We strive to achieve that dream today, and only together will we be successful. It has been 103 days of learning to survive, but together, we did it. Now, we must work to restore the way of life we lost so suddenly.

We will relay any new information as it becomes available through the use of this system.

Thank you, and good night.

It was just over a minute long. Seventy-five seconds to provide the information they'd been waiting 103 days to hear. And yet, there were still a surprising amount of questions.

Where will we go from here? Will we go right back to our dependence on electronics, or will people use a little more caution? Molly wondered. *And what about the more immediate future? When will normal services be restored?*

Burt took charge once again, and elected to cancel classes for the week, in anticipation of the schools reopening. However, Molly discouraged the idea of disassembling the wall in the days immediately following the Restoration. She was concerned that chaos would reign in the outside cities, and felt they needed to stay on guard. She expressed that they needed to stay in check, and remain self-sustaining for the time being, so as not to squander the resources they had worked so hard for. Jimmy agreed, opting to err on the side of caution for now.

Most people concurred, but there were a few who disagreed, and wanted to take the wall down so workers could come into the town and get things up and running fully. Burt considered their suggestion, and decided those who dissented with the way the town was handling the Restoration were free to set up camp outside the wall and wait for the "workers" who would come and offer them salvation, as it were.

Ten people elected to camp on the other side of the wall, waiting for their "salvation." They took enough supplies to last a week, and set up shop within sight of the scouts protecting the wall. The campers were to serve as ambassadors of sorts for the town, and welcome those who would provide information and restore full power to their little corner of the world.

They were dead before the end of the night. Molly was sleeping when she heard it. Her home wasn't even that close to the wall, but she could still hear the screams. They were quiet and distant, but they were there. Dug whined softly upon hearing them.

The next morning, she walked Jimmy's to find out what happened. He told her that a group of Wanderers had come across the campers' site. They were poorly armed, and not anticipating the continued existence of Wanderers once power was restored. So they were slaughtered, and their supplies were taken. There wasn't much the Watchers could do.

"We took out two of them, but not before they killed most of the campers." His voice was tired.

Molly puzzled over it, wondering why the restoration of power hadn't, if not eliminated the Wanderers, then at least lessened their existence so a small group could be safe just outside the gates. Why wouldn't they take shelter somewhere, and take advantage of a life on the verge of being restored? Unless they either didn't know, or couldn't get shelter somewhere. All Molly knew was, they wouldn't be offering any Wanderers shelter anytime soon, that was for sure.

Then she thought of Gary, trying to make his way back home. He was a Wanderer to some people. She thought of his picture on the bulletin board in Burt's basement. But no, he wouldn't kill someone for their food or supplies. He wasn't like that. Molly pictured him deep in the woods, the sun streaming through the treetops. She saw him scrambling around desperately for food, searching for berries, water, anything that would help him sustain his life. In her vision, he was gaunt at best, and appeared to be as desperately clinging to life as his clothing was to his body. She saw him come across a sleeping woman, propping herself up with a backpack, filled with unimaginable treasures. She saw the wild desperation in his eye as he picked up a rock and silently approached her. He quickly dispatched her by bashing her head with the rock and relieved her of everything that might be useful to him, including her clothing. Although she was much smaller than him, an extra layer was an extra layer as the weather became colder. He darted off into the woods with his spoils, not to be seen again.

Molly shuddered at the grim picture she'd created. *What had Gary been through in the last 103 days?* she wondered. She knew she'd done her fair share of things she didn't know she was capable of even considering, in order to survive. What had he done in the name of survival? *Will I still know him? Will he still be the man I loved?* But, more importantly, *Will he make it home?*

As the days passed the town struggled with brownouts. The first blackout happened four days after the Restoration. Panic threatened to settle into the town. The thought that "salvation" had been so fleeting was too much for some folks. There was even a suicide that night.

The next day, Burt held a town meeting in the square and urged calm and patience as the government worked to restore some sense of normalcy. His encouragement was enough to keep most people satisfied at least until the power came back on in limited supply the following day.

However, he was curious about the state of things outside the town walls, and wanted answers for the campers' deaths. So, he organized a reconnaissance group of sorts. Molly immediately volunteered to be part of the group, but was overruled unanimously. Burt explained that after what happened to the campers, they wanted strong, big men who knew how to wield a weapon for this expedition.

Four men were chosen, mostly ones without families or anyone depending too heavily on them. However, most still had important jobs within the community, and if they were killed, the loss would be deeply felt throughout the town. For example, Kevin Murphy had no children and was unmarried, but he lived with his sister's family and helped to maintain the wall as a skilled craftsman. Shane McKenzie was the town's best hunter and often they had him to thank for fresh meat on their tables. Although he was married, he didn't have any children. Clint Black was responsible for making all of the town's tools. He was a blacksmith of sorts. He helped maintain the farming equipment, everything used to build and keep the wall in good shape, everything for hunting and butchering animals. If something was broken, Clint could fix it. But he was single, with no ties to anyone. He lived alone in one of the homes closest to the wall.

And then there was Jimmy. He was selected to be their leader. Just like the others, he had no kids, no family to speak of. But he was pivotal to the town. Only Burt and Molly were totally aware of how much he truly contributed. Not only was he in charge of the Watchers, he was Burt's go-to guy – his unofficial second-in-command. He was the guy Burt always went to for advice, the guy Burt leaned on, the guy who came up with solutions, not questions.

Molly approached him while he was packing a back for the trip. "Jimmy, I wish you wouldn't do this."

He kept packing. "I know you do."

"What if something happens?"

"It won't."

"But where would this town be without you?"

"We'll never know, because I'll be back here later tonight."

She touched his shoulder. "Jimmy."

He turned to face her. "Molly." His expression softened and he shrugged his shoulders. "Look, you only have to manage for a few hours! Burt will be here." He embraced her, and she relished the feeling of safety she always had in his arms. "It'll be OK."

"Promise?"

"I promise."

The expedition made their plans and left first thing the next morning. They planned to be back before dark, so when dark came and went, they all feared the worst. Molly even took a shift on the wall to help watch for them. The next morning, she helped to prepare for the arrival of people with injuries. They sterilized sheets for bandages, tried to gather what was left of their medications and hoped for the best.

They arrived midday. Kevin and Shane carried Clint roughly between the two of them. Kevin had his legs, and Shane had him behind the shoulders. He appeared to be totally unconscious. They were directed to the makeshift hospital and put Clint on the bed closest to the door. Those with more medical knowledge than Molly had descended on him.

Kevin and Shane collapsed in a heap on the other side of the room, well clear of all the action.

She went over and squatted down in front of Shane. He seemed a little dazed, as did Kevin. "What happened?"

"I'm not really sure, it's all such a blur. We ended up going too far to make it home yesterday, so we camped out in the woods." He paused, reliving the memory. "It was just before daybreak when they found us. Looking back on it, it was kind of stupid of them to attack us like that, there were only two of them and four of us. But, one of them managed to do some damage," he gestured towards Clint, "obviously."

"Where's Jimmy?"

Shane glanced around. "He isn't here? He said he'd meet us here. He created a diversion, got the attention of the attackers so Kevin and I could get away with Clint.

We expected him to be here, since he could move faster than us."

Molly tried to process what it all meant. The only definitive thing she could come up with was, "No, he isn't here."

The days passed and Jimmy didn't show up. So Burt decided to hold a town meeting.

They gathered in the square with Burt at center stage. "I'm sorry to say, what little information we were able to gather isn't good."

Murmuring passed like a wave through the crowd, and people shifted their weight uncomfortably.

"It seems," he paused waiting for the murmuring to die down. "The situation is similar to ours in the next closest town – they have a limited power supply, however anarchy has overtaken the fragile balance established during the Blackout. Chaos seems to be running rampant outside our walls. Although there isn't much left to loot, people are stealing from each other, killing for food, lodging and other goods, the list goes on. They are angry at this transitional phase. The general feeling was the power went out in a flash, so when things didn't come back as suddenly, people revolted." He paused, letting people chew on that. "We've paid a high price for this information, and I don't intend to squander it." He paused, collecting himself. "Jimmy, the head of the Watch, is still missing, and presumed dead." His voice cracked a bit when he said "dead."

Molly gasped. Sure, it had been three days he'd been outside the wall, two of them on his own, but he was hearty, and smart about stuff like this. If anyone had a chance out there, it was him. A thought occurred to her. *If Jimmy couldn't even make it out there, how is Gary supposed to?*

Burt interrupted her grim thought. "Although we've had no new information from the radio broadcast, I think it's safe to assume we're still pretty much on our own.

Therefore, I feel we should resume normal operations tomorrow. I also think we should redouble our efforts on the wall. Those of you willing to take an extra shift, please let me know and we will give you a slot. Your efforts will be much appreciated, and may even save lives. At best, it will be an unnecessary precaution. In all honesty, my instincts tell me this will pass rather quickly. Even if they take a while to improve the power grid, people will settle down. This slight change has upset the way of things, but people will adapt more rapidly I think, because the change wasn't as dramatic, and it was a positive change, not a negative as the Blackout was. Please try to remember what we do have. Lights in our homes. Power for our refrigerators and hot water heaters. But more importantly, we have each other." He paused and made eye contact with Molly. "Together, we will get through this uncertain time, the same way we got through the first days of the Blackout." He paused, surveying the uncertain faces in the crowd. "Are there any questions?"

Molly had a million questions, but they were all jumbled up in this new information they thought would be more hopeful than it was. "OK, well, let's get to work," Burt said.

With that, their lives changed again, and yet somehow they stayed woefully the same.

39.

Fifteen days after the lights came back on, Gary was achingly close to home. He estimated only two or three more days left in the journey. While they were trotting along through the woods on that fifteenth day, it occurred to him that Molly and he could have settled down anywhere. They could have taken that job in Miami, and she could be living there now. That would've added another two weeks or more to the trip. *Holy crap I'm glad we didn't take that job,* he thought. *Or, I could've had a flight to the Bahamas that fateful day. Then what would I have done, with sixty miles of deep blue sea between the two of us?* Considering all the ways this could have played out, what happened wasn't the most ideal, but it wasn't the worst-case scenario either, at least not yet.

The days after the Restoration were much like the ones that preceded it, at least for Gary. He heard whispers of total chaos in the beginning, and kept to the deep woods after that first night on the edge of Plymouth.

He noticed the Wanderers were getting more bold and violent. Just a few days after the Restoration, he was walking deep in the woods when he came upon a grisly scene that could only be blamed on Wanderers. The poor couple's bodies had been stripped and there was blood everywhere. It looked like the woman's head had been bashed in, and the man had been stabbed with something jagged. The blood was making Thunderbolt nervous, so they didn't linger. Gary couldn't decide if he was happy or sad that he'd come upon them after their demise. He wasn't sure there was anything he could've done for them.

And who's to say they wouldn't have taken me for all I was worth once the danger to them was passed? It wasn't the most idealistic way to think, but it was keeping him alive for the time being. That night, they walked further than normal, trying to put as much distance as possible between them and the unfortunate couple.

They did fairly well staying away from people when they didn't want to be seen, and after about a week, he ventured a little closer to a town he was passing by to try and get an update on the situation. It seemed like things had quieted down, but normal operations were far from being restored. At best, the lights were on; at worst, transportation services, phone services and things of that nature were a long way from being useful. So, the lights were on, but people felt like it'd been false hope because no additional improvements followed.

The anger in the area was down to a simmer, but Gary felt like he was in a pressure cooker. Before long, he worried it would explode. The pair continued on their steady trot home, and Gary prayed they would make it before that happened.

40.

It had been eighteen days since The Restoration. Jimmy had not come back. Molly couldn't ignore the fact that her dear friend was probably dead, although she would never know for sure.

About a week after Burt's announcement, Molly held a memorial for him. Not many people came, which didn't surprise her. He'd kept a pretty low profile in the town, and stayed standoffish with most people. Burt came and said a few words, and all the Watchers who weren't working came, but they stayed quiet.

She'd spent some time sitting in his house, hoping he would come back. After about a week of doing that after school, she finally took his radio over to her house. She knew he'd want her to have it. He was always looking out for her.

At home, listening to the loop feed, she gave in to the despondency. Her rock was gone. Gary wasn't there. How was she supposed to go on?

Beth did what she could to comfort her, but death is always difficult to understand for an outsider.

The town struggled to get back to "normal" without him. The Watch suffered from disorganization at a critical time. They'd had two near-breeches of the wall since Jimmy's disappearance, but each time they'd learned from their mistakes.

Burt tried to stay busy, moving from task to task with little emotion spent on any one thing.

They had lights intermittently, they could take showers in their homes, and even had hot water some of the time – that was Molly's favorite luxury. She'd gotten used to using candles, but the sheer extravagance of a hot, indoor shower was amazing. The first time, just after the Restoration, she stood there for a half hour just marveling at how good it felt, and trying to wash away some of the things that had happened in the last three months.

But, nearly a month after the power had returned, they finally settled back into a routine. The kids were back in school at Molly's house, and the patrol was back to its normal operations. They even elected a new leader who seemed to be doing a fair job. Really, everything was back to the way it was during the Blackout, they just had lights and hot water.

A few days before, the broadcast had been updated, but it wasn't great news.

My Fellow Americans,

It's been fifteen days since the Restoration, and we're saddened to say many have not heeded our requests to stay calm and continue your normal operations. It would seem chaos has reigned in many areas around the country. The military has been able to organize a small force around the capital to protect what's left of the government there and maintain a certain amount of order. However, at this point in time, there are not enough resources to help you all. Therefore, you must help yourselves. Return your towns to civilization promptly.

Reports of brownouts and blackouts continue to filter in. The grid is far from stable, but be encouraged by the fact that every day improvements are made.

Questions are circulating regarding the restoration of transportation and communication services. Unfortunately there is no word on when help in those areas may come.

For now, that is all. Good night.

It was really nothing they didn't already know. It took fifteen days for them to regurgitate information that was already old news. Nothing had changed when it came to the government.

So, by the time day eighteen rolled around, Molly had worked hard to settle back into her routines and not think about Gary or Jimmy. Because transportation systems weren't up and running, she told herself it was no surprise Gary hadn't made it home yet. And just because the lights were back on, he still had no way of calling or getting in touch at all. Just because there was nothing but silence for 121 days, didn't mean he was never coming home. Just because Jimmy didn't, didn't mean Gary wouldn't.

It was cold comfort at night when the only warm body she shared the bed with was Dug, who slept by her feet.

That day, they were studying *Pride and Prejudice*, by one of the girls' request. Molly promised the boys they could pick the next one, and it sounded like it would be *Dracula*. She was certain the girls would love that about as much as the boys loved *Pride and Prejudice*, but it gave them all something to look forward to, and she liked that they were staying involved.

"So, do you think if someone were to write a story like this today it would still be relevant? Do you think it would be as timeless as Austen's story?" Molly asked.

"No," one of the boys immediately chimed in.

"Why not, Stuart?" He was a short, freckled brunet boy about fourteen years old – a little young for the subject matter, but mature for his age, so she thought he could handle it. He was also one of the boys spearheading the Dracula campaign.

"Because it doesn't work like that anymore. Families aren't indebted to each other like that, for one thing. And daughters aren't as much of a burden either. The things they struggled with are different than the things families struggle with today."

"OK, that's a valid point. So, what would a modern-day Elizabeth and Darcy struggle with?"

Samantha, an eager blonde-headed girl about sixteen, raised her hand. "Elizabeth in her time wasn't very accomplished. I think a modern day *Pride and Prejudice* Elizabeth would have the opposite problem. She would still struggle with pride, she would just have more material things to be proud of. Today's woman is very successful and some men feel threatened by that, and are even prejudiced against feminists. I think that's where their struggles would be. Darcy wouldn't be prejudiced against her station as a poor person, he'd be prejudiced against her station as a high-powered executive and the stigma that goes along with that."

It was very insightful for a sixteen-year-old. Molly wondered what would become of her in this new world. "So, post-Blackout and Restoration, where do you think Elizabeth and Darcy fit in?"

No one answered. They all seemed unsure, and a few of them were frowning. Others were picking at the grass. Molly had asked a question they weren't sure they wanted to hear the answer to. "This is where relevancy becomes an issue, I think. Today's couple, and family for that matter, is focused on survival. They're not caught up in issues of pride and prejudice. They're worried about how to feed themselves, how to keep warm, and how to stay alive until tomorrow." They were silent. It wasn't a subject they liked to dwell on. She smiled in an effort to comfort them. "But I don't think it will always be this way. A civilization can't sustain itself in survival mode forever. It will either adapt, or destroy itself. As we've continued to adapt throughout the ages, I think we will follow suit here, and Austen's work will become relevant again, if not slightly out of date."

A few of them smiled, feeling encouraged. "Mrs. Bonham?" Niles, a quiet boy in the back called out.

"Yes?"

"When do you think we will adapt?"

Molly frowned. "I don't know. It's easy to look back on history and see a dark time as a single page in a book, isn't it? But for the ones living it, that could have been years of their life summed up in a single paragraph. All I know for certain is that it can't stay like this forever, and within your lifetime it will get better if you set your minds to it."

A few heads nodded, and she watched their wheels start turning. "OK, that's probably enough for right now. Let's take a break, and then we'll do a bit of science."

There was a low *yesss* that they apparently thought was in an octave Molly couldn't hear. She smiled as she turned back towards the house. That's when she saw Burt standing on the back porch.

"Molly. Something's happened."

41.

Seventeen days after the Restoration, Gary closed in on his hometown. He came to a small clearing in the woods and discovered a man lying on his stomach motionless. He considered moving on, but then wondered what would've happened to him if Judd had done the same. He was close enough to home now he may be able to help, if the man was still alive.

He climbed down from Thunderbolt's back and approached the man quietly, the knife Judd had given him at the ready.

"Hey." He said as he knelt beside him. There was no response. He grabbed the man's shoulder over his dark brown coat. "Hey. You alright?" Nothing. He pulled his collar down a little to feel for a pulse. As soon as he touched the cold skin, he knew he would find nothing. He did feel something bumpy and equally cold. A chain.

He rolled the man over and was startled by his expression. His skin was a sickly yellow color, and he had a dark beard. He was middle aged, maybe in his late fifties or early sixties. His eyes were what bothered Gary the most. They seemed familiar as they stared blankly at Gary.

He reached into the man's collar to see if he could free the chain. Dog tags. *Let's find out who you are.*

JEAN JAMES M
SSN 314-58-9045
O-

Gary's heart sunk. *Jimmy.* He collapsed back staring at the tags in his hand. He looked from the tags to Jimmy. *There must be some mistake. What was he doing out here?* He put his head in his hands and cried, pressing Jimmy's tags into his forehead. *How could this happen?*

He wasn't sure how long he let himself mourn. Eventually he dragged the back of his arm across his face, and resolved himself to the task at hand. He couldn't just leave him like that. He set about burying Jimmy with what little resources he had. He didn't have a shovel or anything to dig with, so he resolved to collect rocks, pine needles and branches to cover him. It took the rest of the day, and he was exhausted when it was done. But, this man – the first person Gary had come into contact with from his past in nearly four months – was laid to rest.

That night, Gary laid down next to him and slept like the dead company he kept.

The next day, he reached the outer limits of his hometown. As he approached, a wall rose up from the horizon.

He frowned. *This could be problematic.*

He referenced the map and surroundings. Everything was wilder than it was when he was there last, but he knew he was in the right place. *They must've put the wall up after the Blackout.* He tried not to think too hard about what might have prompted its construction.

As he got closer, he opted to go to the road, thinking that's where the gate might be. He also didn't want to look like he was being sneaky. He could see movement at the top of the wall, and could only assume they had a patrol set up – most likely to keep Wanderers like him on the right side of the wall. He felt confident though that if he made himself known, he could explain who he was.

Heck, maybe I'd even be recognized. He hoped. He and Molly weren't overly involved in neighborhood activities, especially him since he was home so intermittently, but maybe he'd get lucky. Maybe Molly would be one of the ones patrolling the wall. The adrenaline rush from the prospect of seeing Molly for the first time in 121 days gave him strength.

So, Gary and Thunderbolt trotted boldly up to the wall. That was when it started to go wrong.

42.

Molly glanced over at Beth and she told her group to work out the problems on page thirty-six, and hurried over. They approached Burt together.

"What's going on?" Molly asked.

"The Watchers have caught someone. A Wanderer."

"Oh, well that's great! Do they think it's one of the ones responsible for the campers? Or is it one of the ones who attacked Jimmy?" Molly asked.

"No. It's not any of them. Although I had to do some pretty fast talking to convince some of the Watchers of that."

Molly was confused. "So…why hold him then? What do you plan to do with him, Burt? Ya gonna put him to work here?"

"Well, he'll have to find some way to contribute if he wants to stay here."

Beth had had enough. "For heaven's sake Burt, who is it?"

Burt looked hard at Molly. "It's Gary."

43.

"STOP!" Someone shouted from the wall. Gary obliged them, not wanting any trouble.

"Move along. We don't want any trouble from the likes of you," someone else said. Gary didn't recognize their voices, which didn't give him a warm fuzzy.

"I actually live here. Would you mind letting me in?" What else was he going to say?

"This guy thinks he's funny. Hey Shane, come over here! We've got a comedian on our hands!"

The second guy piped up. He seemed a little more level-headed than the first guy goading him on. "Please, buddy. We don't want an altercation here. Just move on. Wanderers aren't welcome here."

"But I'm not a Wanderer!"

The first guy notched an arrow and aimed it at Gary. "Perhaps we're not being clear."

"No, please! I'm married to Molly Bonham! Just go get her! You don't have to bring me inside unless she says so."

The second one put his hand on the deadly arrow and forced the first guy to lower it. He examined Gary for a minute, puzzled. "Molly's husband?" Gary saw him give a signal to another Watcher – a barely noticeable head nod in the other direction. "We'll just see about that."

Before Gary knew it, a group of men closed in around him and his horse. He got off Thunderbolt in an attempt to prove he meant no harm, but it provided them with the opportunity they were waiting for. They seized Gary, put a burlap sack on his head and tied his hands behind his back. They lead him roughly through the gate, a man on each side.

Gary turned and struggled a bit when they started leading him away. "Thunderbolt!"

"We've got your horse. And we'll put him to good use. Consider it payment for entertaining this charade."

Then he was led away.

44.

Molly's breathing quickened and her heart raced. She kept hearing Burt's voice over and over again. *It's Gary... It's Gary ... It's Gary ...*

She didn't remember the walk to the house where they were keeping him. She couldn't believe it. *But if it wasn't Gary, who was it? It has to be him.* When the house came in sight, she started running.

"Molly!" Burt called out.

She burst through the door, out of breath. She expected him to be there, in front of her, arms open, but there was no one. She frantically went from room to room searching for him, calling his name.

Eventually Burt caught up. "He's in the basement, Molly. Remember what we agreed to do when we found Wanderers?"

She grunted and took the stairs two at a time. She tripped when she was almost to the basement door and skinned her knee pretty good, but didn't feel it. She scrambled to her feet and darted to the stairwell.

She stood in front of it, not sure she wanted to see what was down there. *What if it's not him? What if he'd changed so much that he won't be happy with me anymore? What if ... What if it is him and we can have our life back?*

She slowly took the steps down into the darkness.

45.

Suddenly, she was there, standing at the bottom of the steps. The light from above shined on her, giving her an angelic appearance.

"Gary? Oh my God! Are you OK?" There was an edge to her voice, like she was barely holding it together.

She looked him over hesitantly. In the months since the Blackout his hair had gotten long, he'd grown a beard and lost a lot of weight. To be honest, he was quite feral-looking. But then, she didn't look the same to him either. Her clothes were worn, her hair had lost its luster, and if possible she'd gotten thinner than Gary had ever seen her. The Blackout had been hard on both of them.

"Molly," he breathed. He moved to go to her, but couldn't. His hands were tied behind the chair, preventing escape.

She closed the distance between them. "Gary!" She threw her arms around him and all he wanted to do was reciprocate. He struggled against his bindings.

One of his captors cleared his throat. "So, this is Gary for sure?" Gary had forgotten they were even there.

She pulled away and looked deep into his eyes. A beautiful smile spread across her face as she gently smoothed his beard. "Yes. It's him. My husband has come home."

Burt cut his restraints and Gary hugged her like never before. It was then that she started to cry. Burt clapped a hand on Gary's shoulder while he embraced his wife, smiled knowingly, and ushered the other men out of the basement. For the first time in 121 days, Gary was alone with the love of his life, and he held on to that moment with everything he had.

46.

"We come to beginnings only at the end."
– William Throsby Bridges

Did you enjoy this book?
Let the author know!
Leave a review online!

The following is an excerpt from Stephanie Erickson's latest post-apocalyptic novel, <u>The Dead Room</u>.

Approx. 322 years after the apocalypse

1.

The body lay on a two-piece metal pyre in the center of the clearing. Nothing more than the skeleton of a table, the pyre was simply used for the display and transport of the bodies. Burning the dead was a custom from the time before.

The corpse's blue cotton, long-sleeved shirt was buttoned all the way to the top to hide his injuries, and the matching navy slacks had recently been pressed. With his hands folded over his abdomen, Wesley looked rather dashing. Ashley wished her match had actually been dashing in life.

She wondered who would wear that outfit next. Nothing was ever wasted on the island. Not even the clothes of a dead man. She herself had worn the clothes off a dead woman's back. Squeamishness was a luxury no one could afford.

Although "new" clothes were made on the island, from animal skins and the cotton grown in the farmlands, they were typically reserved for the higher ups—elders, doctors, and the like. Cotton was difficult to grow in the cold climate, and the clothes were made entirely by hand. Once it had been worn and patched a few times by those with power, new clothing was eventually passed down to the lower branches of society,

But, it wasn't just clothing that moved on after an islander died. All of their belongings were redistributed among those in need. The dead's family wasn't allowed to keep anything they didn't need. Sentimentality was a lost emotion to the islanders. Reusing everything was essential, even if the previous owner was a dead man.

It had only bothered her once—the first time she'd seen one of her father's outfits on another man. Even then, at the tender age of ten, she'd understood it was bound to happen eventually. She just hadn't expected it to happen so quickly. Only a week after his funeral, she'd spotted one of her neighbors walking down the road in her father's clothes. She ran to him, hoping her father's scent might still linger on his shirt. But the man neither embraced her nor offered her any sympathy. He only looked at her with wide eyes, the horror and disgust plain on his face.

Death on the island was such a strange thing. She'd lost track of how many funerals she'd been to in her lifetime—at least one a month. Unexpected deaths, like that of her match, added to the average.

Only three of the losses had actually meant something to her—her mother, her father, and now Wesley. Her father's funeral was, of course, devastating, made more so by the fact that they'd shared the same first name. Everything the elders said about him could have also been applied to her. How they were thankful for "Ashley's life," how they wished "Ashley peace." It sent shivers down her spine.

Once, she'd asked him why they shared a name. His mother's name had been Ashley, he'd explained, as had her mother, and her father before that. On and on, down the line, the name had traveled, until it had reached Ashley. And one day, as was their tradition, it would go to her own child.

The funeral for her mother, who had been taken by a simple cold that escalated into something much worse, was nothing more than a hazy memory. Still, Ashley missed her mother terribly and felt incomplete without her. She searched for her whenever the jasmine got caught on the wind, because her mother had loved to wear the flower behind her ear.

Wesley's funeral was a problem. She wasn't entirely sure how she felt about it. The loss of her parents had left her feeling completely alone. She'd hoped to find love again with her match, but he'd left her terribly disappointed.

Now that he was gone, her emotions warred with themselves. Relief was the biggest player fighting for space in her mind. Relief to have escaped the abuse and the pressures of being the next elder's wife. Guilt came in at a close second, but not because she regretted killing her match.

It was because her best friend was being blamed for it.

She sat alone in the front row, worrying her hands as she took in the scene around her. A large crowd was gathered in a semi-circle around the body. The clearing was equipped with seating for roughly a thousand people, and the island's population tended to hover near that number, plus or minus ten or fifteen people. Wesley had been such a prominent figure in their community—next in line to be an elder—so nearly the whole island had come to pay their respects. Most of those present had always told Ashley that she was so lucky to be matched with him.

If that's luck, they can keep it, she thought. *Funny how relaxed and peaceful he looks now,* Ashley mused as she studied his body. She snorted, causing pain to shoot through her right side where he'd kicked her last night.

She grimaced, and her hand automatically flew to the spot. *Was it really just last night?* she marveled. So much had happened.

The summer had been warm that year, warmer than normal for the northwestern island, but a crisp taste of fall was on the wind. In a vain attempt to keep out the cold, and the memories, she adjusted her shawl around her shoulders. A breeze rustled the spruce trees bordering the circular clearing, ruffling it back out of place.

The islanders in the rows surrounding Ashley watched her as she fidgeted. They probably assumed she was in shock. Maybe she was. Memories of her match flooded her mind. She knew from the start that she didn't love him, but love wasn't the point of matches—continuing the species was.

Her life had become so much worse, though, after learning who Wesley really was—nothing but rage. She couldn't get her mind around how badly the elders had misjudged him. Or maybe she was the one they'd misjudged.

The memories continued to close in on her like the evening fog, until she reached the night before. The hits, the kicks, and the ugly words all flashed in her mind. She felt every strike land on her a second time. Felt her hand take the knife…

Her heart raced, and her breath came in short gasps. Tears streamed down her face. Taking a deep breath, she tried to steady herself. She couldn't afford to panic. The others might suspect something, and then what? Though she could think of no possible way things could get worse than they already were, her lack of imagination was undoubtedly born of grief—not for her dead match, but for her best friend, her only family, who was awaiting his execution.

Before she could dwell on Mason's fate, the funeral service started.

Elder Alkoff led the procession, with Elder Mattli and the other seven elders in tow. Dressed in funeral robes that covered their arms and dragged on the ground behind them, they all walked down the center aisle, heads bowed. None had their hoods raised, as was customary for funeral services. The elders thought it would comfort the islanders to look upon the faces of their leaders in such a dark moment.

Elder Alkoff clutched the book as he made his way toward the body, his black robe kicking out in front of him. When he arrived at the pyre, he paused, muttered a few words, and turned to face the crowd. The rest of the elders spread out on either side of him, forming a row.

Opening the book to the proper section automatically, Alkoff didn't even look at it when he spoke. He'd conducted enough funerals to know the words by heart, and so he kept his tired, gray eyes trained on the islanders. "In the name of our savior, Bennett Ashby, we give thanks for this life. For without him, it would not have existed at all." His voice was deep, booming, and authoritative, echoing across the clearing.

The crowd responded as one, "We thank you for this life, Bennett Ashby."

As Alkoff continued the service, Ashley wondered what that even meant. Were they thanking Bennett Ashby for their own lives, or for her match's? She certainly wasn't thankful for his life. And just then, she wasn't sure she was all that thankful for her own.

"We continue to give thanks and praise for this island, and all the lives on it, for we have been spared the horrible fate of those who came before."

The crowd responded, "We give thanks and praise to you, our savior, Bennett Ashby."

Again, Ashley's mind wandered. What exactly was the 'horrible fate' the elders so often referred to? Could it be worse than submitting to an abusive man in the name of continuing the species? All the elders ever said was that civilization had crumbled at its own hands, and the islanders were the only survivors. No one knew more than that, but to hear the elders tell it, the island was the only part of the world that was still inhabited. But Ashley had a hard time accepting that as truth. What made the island so special that only they had been chosen to survive?

She shook her head. *Now's not the time for that train of thought.*

By the time Ashley tuned back in, Alkoff had closed the book and moved on with the ceremony. Elder Mattli stepped forward.

Alkoff's second in command cleared his throat in preparation for his part of the ceremony. "Wesley was…" he paused briefly, "…full of potential. The elders would have had a strong ally in him. His presence will be missed." He let out a short sigh when he was done.

He turned to the body and sprinkled a handful of sand on it. "Ashes to ashes, dust to dust. So we return this body to the Earth."

Do they really return the bodies to the Earth? Ashley wondered, not for the first time. No one was allowed to see what the elders did with the bodies after a funeral. The body was carried away by two of the elders. The clothing, along with the rest of Wesley's extraneous belongings that Ashley didn't need, would later be delivered to its next owners by one of the elders' lackeys. There were no graveyards on the island—the space couldn't be spared—and Ashley didn't remember ever seeing smoke after a funeral. *Maybe they dump them into the sea.* She imagined a huge skeleton reef offshore with centuries of bodies in various stages of decomposition. The image was grotesquely comedic, and she stifled what would've been a manic laugh.

Mattli returned to his place among the elders as Alkoff continued the ceremony. "Through death comes life." The crowd stirred with anticipation of who would be allowed—or forced, depending on how you looked at it—to add to the population now that a death had occurred. "Constance and Matthew Deneau, we look forward to celebrating the life you can now bring into this world."

A collective sigh passed over the crowd, and a few people patted Matthew on the shoulder to give him their silent congratulations. Ashley eyed Constance, trying to decide if she was happy or not. She didn't know the girl very well, but they were about the same age. With both of them in their mid-twenties, they were an ideal age to contribute to the population.

But Ashley wondered how fulfilling that would even be. Childbirth was dangerous on the island, and not without peril. Worse, illness was hard on children, and some never made it to adulthood. The island's finite population made inbreeding a problem, and babies were often stillborn or born with deformities they didn't survive. Legends were shared of a time when medicine had been plentiful, and disease more sophisticated than a respiratory infection, but life was smaller on the island. A common cold was all it took to snuff out a little one.

Mattli caught her eye, bringing her back to the service. "Now go in peace, knowing that as one life ends, another begins. So it is for you."

So it is for me, huh? she asked herself. *What could my life possibly hold now?* She despaired as the crowd slowly filed away, leaving her alone and trapped between her future and her past.

Ashley continued to sit, staring at her match's body. By the time she felt Mattli take her hand, she was numb, whether from the cold or the events of the last twenty-four hours, she wasn't sure.

"My dear. You should go home. It's getting cold." His hands were wrinkled by time, but they were warm and comforting as they enveloped hers.

"I'd like to stay with him. To know what happens to him." She didn't finish her thought out loud. *Since I don't know what my own future holds.*

"I'm afraid that's not possible." It was a simple, firm answer. But Ashley couldn't accept it.

Anger rose inside of her, surprising her with its intensity. Everything was so chaotic, and she felt this was one thing she should've been able to control. She clawed at the opportunity desperately. "He was my match. I have a right to see him laid to rest." Her voice echoed off the canopy of trees above them.

Mattli's eyes turned sad. "Yes, you do. But I'm afraid you just can't. You know that. You've been here before."

That was true enough. She wasn't an elder, but she could probably go through the service from memory.

But this one was different. She would not miss Wesley, but in many ways, his death signified the end of her life. She was nothing to the island without her match. They needed every young woman to produce more hands to help till the earth, repair buildings and machines, keep records, and keep the island running. The child's sex didn't matter—more bodies were what they needed. It was her most important role. Yes, she was also responsible for mending and making fishing nets on the island, and she was good at it too. But continuing the species was everyone's top priority. And now that opportunity was likely lost to her.

Though she wouldn't have wanted Wesley's children, she was unhappy to have lost her main purpose.

Mattli stood, and she followed automatically, not consciously processing her actions. "Ashley, you are young and fertile. You may yet be rematched."

She shuddered at the thought. That wasn't what she wanted at all. But she didn't know what she *did* want. The future looked bleak, especially if she'd have to spend it without Mason.

"At any rate, my dear, you aren't a lost soul. The island

can't afford lost souls. You know that. You'll find your purpose, and it will be soon." An 'or else' hung in the air between them, making Ashley uneasy.

Her response caught in her throat when she realized the elder had walked her home. Feeling deflated, her shoulders sagged.

"Go get some rest. In the morning, it will be over."

She nearly crumpled, knowing exactly what 'it' referred to. Her best friend's wrongful execution would be far more difficult to endure than her match's funeral.

The Dead Room is available now on _Amazon.com_.

ACKNOWLEDGMENTS

"In daily life we must see that it is not happiness that makes us grateful, but gratefulness that makes us happy."
— Brother David Steindl-Rast

First, I would like to thank God. I know that sounds cheesy and cliché, but we've been given so many blessings lately I can't help but feel awed and grateful.

Of course, thank you to my wonderful husband for giving me the idea for this book. But thank you most of all for providing me with the opportunity to write it. I hope you like it after all this work!

Thanks to my family for all of your support, help tweaking and overall cheerleading. To my cousin Jamie, for reading a very early draft and helping point me in better directions. Thank you Larry, my father-in-law, for providing me with a never-ending stream of research! You made my life so much easier. Shane, my brother, I swear, if I have to hear that freaking *Family Guy* quote about that novel I'm writing one more time, you may die in the next one. You've been warned. Dad, your love and support are unceasing. I wouldn't be here without your constant faith in my ability to succeed. Mom, my ideal reader, thank you for going to the Young Author's Conference with me in fifth grade. Thank you for always believing this is what I was made to do. Thank you for reading, re-reading, critiquing, and tweaking. Thank you for knowing exactly when to say, "You know what honey, this isn't your best." Or, "Holy cow, this is amazing, quit messing with it." I love you the mostest.

To my friend Mary, you are amazing. Everyone should have a cheerleader like you in their life. Jean and Jim, you were so helpful and inspirational for this book. Cindy, HL and Doris, thank you for your love and support. I hope the book lives up to your expectations! All my friends at the Morningside Writer's Group, thank you for teaching me about what criticism to listen to, and what to ignore. You guys are awesome!

My editor, Alexis Arendt of Word Vagabond, you really helped turn this book into something special. Without you, I don't think it would've made it past the first draft. You are an absolute gem.

Lastly, thanks to you, reader. I know your time is extremely valuable, and I thank you for sharing some of it with me.

ABOUT THE AUTHOR

Stephanie Erickson graduated from Flagler College in St. Augustine, Florida with a Bachelor of Arts degree in English Literature. Post graduation, she became a graphic designer, and only recently has been afforded the opportunity to get back into writing. She currently lives with her husband in Port St. Lucie, Florida. The couple is expecting their first child in March of 2013. *The Blackout* is Stephanie's first novel.

43180589R00136

Made in the USA
Lexington, KY
21 July 2015